Praise *for* the work of Sandra Steffen

"Steffen is one of those authors whose characters and their emotions ring true, which makes each book a heartfelt treat."
   —*Romantic Times*

"Steffen's characters are thoroughly and thoughtfully conceived…the charm of this tale lies in her lovely portrayal of complex family relationships."
   —*Publishers Weekly* on *The Cottage*

"Sandra Steffen is a veritable master at creating characters. On a scale of 1–10, a 15!"
   —*ReaderToReader.com*

"Steffen knows exactly how hard to tug on readers' heart-strings for maximum effect."
   —*Booklist*

"Warm, unforgettable characters come to life in Sandra's small-town setting."
   —*Round Table Reviews* on *Come Summer*

"A compelling, heartwarming tale. Steffen is a talented author to watch."
   —Bestselling author Kat Martin on *The Cottage*

"A charming, intense story. High drama and gentle reflection—the perfect mix."
   —Bestselling author Stella Cameron on *The Cottage*

"A powerfully riveting story that pulls the reader from page one and doesn't stop…one of the most original plots I've ever seen…flawless characterization."
   —*Romance Reviews Today* on *Come Summer*

Sandra Steffen

Sandra Steffen has always been a storyteller. She began nurturing this hidden talent by concocting adventures for her brothers and sisters, even though the boys were more interested in her ability to hit a baseball over the barn—an automatic home run. She didn't begin her pursuit of publication until she was a young wife and mother of four sons. Since her thrilling debut as a published author in 1992, thirty-three of her novels have graced bookshelves across the country.

Professional reviewers have called Sandra a veritable master at creating characters, and her books well written, satisfying and intelligent. Her most cherished review came from her youngest son recently when he said, "Mom, I hear your voice as I'm reading your book."

This winner of the RITA® Award, the Wish Award, and the National Readers Choice Award enjoys traveling with her husband. Usually their destinations are settings for her upcoming books. They are empty nesters these days. Who knew it could be so much fun? Please visit her at www.sandrasteffen.com.

Life happens

SANDRA STEFFEN

LIFE HAPPENS

copyright © 2005 Sandra E. Steffen

isbn 037388060X

This edition published by arrangement with Harlequin Books S.A.

® and TM are trademarks of the publisher. Trademarks indicated with
® are registered in the United States Patent and Trademark Office, the
Canadian Trade Marks Office and in other countries.

TheNextNovel.com

HARLEQUIN®

PRINTED IN U.S.A.

From the Author

Dear Reader Friends,

I hope you enjoy *Life Happens*. I won't apologize if this story makes you cry. If it does, I would have to apologize for making you smile, too. It's human nature to feel as though laughter is somehow our due and tears our punishment, but aren't both part of life?

The idea for *Life Happens* woke me from a deep sleep and came to me complete with a beginning, a middle and an end. It was the first time it had happened this way. From the moment of its conception, I knew I had to tell this poignant story, which began as a tribute to my beloved brother, who died on a blustery night in 1995. The details that led to that day aren't unique: the diagnosis, the prayers, the bone-marrow transplant that failed, the hole his death left in our family. Just as losing Ron taught me more about life than death, *Life Happens* became a story about life, too, and the bond between a mother and child, and a man and a woman, a bond so strong it waited nearly two decades to spring up, so fierce it was painful and so full of hope and joy it became a power unto itself.

Like so many of life's mysteries, *Life Happens* was a blessing in disguise, for it has led me down this path to this moment. I've been blessed many times over, with family and friends, laughter and luck, and with this gift I've been given that wakes me in the middle of the night with stories that insist upon being written. There is one more blessing I can't fail to mention, and that blessing is you, dear reader friends.

Until next time and always...

Sandra

In loving memory of my brother, and all our brothers—
and sisters—who've fought life's battles and lost,
and for all those who've won.

"The highest reward for your toil is not what you get
for it but what you become of it."—John Ruskin

CHAPTER 1

Mya Donahue felt naked. And not in a good way.

What had she done?

Most of her hair, her beautiful, long, lustrous hair, was gone. What was left stuck out in four- and five-inch tufts, as if she'd gotten caught in some cosmic blender. She turned her head slightly. It was no use. It looked bad from every angle.

What had she been thinking?

She could have blamed it on the weather. For generations, the descendants of the Irishmen and Scotsmen who'd settled along this stretch of the rocky coast of Maine had insisted that days like this were at the root of all evil. The day *was* wet, windy and a little wild, but to blame? It wasn't the weather. More likely it was the month. April was always a dangerous time for her.

"A trim?" Rolf had asked when she'd arrived at the trendy hair salon located directly above Brynn's, her clothing boutique in Portland's waterfront district.

For weeks she'd been watching Rolf's clients traipse past her display windows, looking, if not gorgeous, at the very least fresh and totally transformed. During the lull after lunch today, Mya had flipped the Closed sign in the window and crept upstairs. Shutting the door on a gust of wind and the bawl of a far-off foghorn that sounded suspiciously like the voice of reason, she'd heard herself say, "Surprise me."

Surprise me? Had she lost her mind?

Mya loved new trends: clunky-heeled shoes and boots of all kinds, low-slung pants and the latest jewelry. But other than an occasional trim, she never changed her hairstyle. Until today.

Even the window-shoppers and early tourists who'd never seen her before had watched her closely the rest of the day. Those who knew her were downright blunt.

"Whoa," her after-school clerk exclaimed.

"You cut your hair!" the woman who owned the bookstore next door had said, in case Mya didn't know.

Joe, the kindly deliveryman said, "Don't worry. It'll grow back."

By the end of the afternoon, Mya had been ready to tell even the paying customers to stick their opinions. The old Mya would have. But the new Mya didn't. The new and improved, cool, calm and collected Mya counted to ten and clenched so hard she nearly cracked a tooth.

Looking at her reflection in the safety of her own living room, she pulled at the wayward tresses. It was no use. She turned her back on the baroque mirror. Beseeching her two closest friends, she said, "What do you think?"

"Did you consult the personal emotional tides of the moon chart I gave you last Christmas?" Suzette Lewis asked.

Mya all but dropped her face into her hands. Until she'd met Suzette, the only thing she'd known about her astrological sign was that she was an Aries. "Do I look like I consulted anything?"

Suzette studied the uneven blond tendrils encircling Mya's head. Petite and at times just a little too perky, Suzette said, "It isn't that bad."

Coming from Sunny Suzie, that meant it wasn't that good, either. The accompanying smile was a bold-faced lie.

"Claire?" Mya asked the other woman.

As droll as Suzette was sunny, Claire O'Brien wore her dark hair long and loose, much the way she wore her clothes. Unlike Mya and Suzette, Claire wasn't from Maine. Originally from upstate New York, there was something mysterious about her. Mya had never had a truer friend, or a more honest one, which Claire proved when she said, "In the future, I wouldn't change your hairstyle the same week you become engaged."

Suzette dropped into an overstuffed chair. "I still can't believe you're engaged." Not many thirty-year-old women could pull off that whine. "I'm the one who's always dreamed of marrying a doctor. It was my appendix that ruptured."

Fighting queasiness, Mya muttered, "Don't say ruptured."

Pouting, Suzette said, "Fine. It was my appendix that *ex-*

panded violently, and who was just coming off duty in E.R.? Only the best-looking doctor in the English-speaking world."

Mya stopped tugging at her hair long enough to admit that Jeffrey *was* incredibly good-looking, although *that* wasn't why she'd started seeing him.

"You're right, Suzette," Claire said from the sofa. "It was terribly inconsiderate of Mya to answer her phone in the dead of night when you called, sobbing. And it was thoughtless of her to throw on her clothes, brave a blinding snowstorm and her fear of hospitals and drive you to the Emergency Room, then wait not only until you came out of surgery, but until you were out of recovery, too."

"Gosh, when you put it that way, maybe Mya does deserve that two-karat rock more than I do, even though I *am* the one who had emergency surgery. But Claire, she doesn't even *care* about diamonds."

Mya could only shrug, because it was true. Most of the time, she forgot the ring was there, which explained the fast little jolt she felt each time she caught the flash of it in her peripheral vision. She'd only been engaged for four days. Surely, she would get used to it.

"Where is the groom-to-be, anyway?" Suzette asked.

The door opened, and the three friends turned with varying degrees of interest. Mya was the only one who groaned, for it wasn't Jeffrey at all.

"The cavalry to the rescue," Claire said under her breath.

Never one to waste the spotlight, Mya's mother lowered her umbrella and beamed all around. "Everyone I've talked to today has had it, HAD IT with this weather. That's some dice-job, Mya."

What little hair was left on the back of Mya's neck stood on end. "This dice-job cost me eighty bucks."

The older woman answered without missing a beat. "Which only proves what I've always said. Just because something's more expensive doesn't mean it's better. Now let's have a closer look."

Mya had little choice but to succumb to the inspection that followed. After much tongue clicking and head shaking, her mother rummaged through her big, red purse for a pair of red-tipped scissors. Red was her mother's favorite color. She wore red nail polish, red lipstick, red blush on her cheeks, red shoes, red everything. Even her '95 Impala was red.

"Well? What do you think?" Mya asked.

"I think you paid too much. I only charge my customers twenty dollars for a shampoo, cut and blow job."

Suzette gasped. Claire smirked. And Mya said, "I believe you mean blow-dry, Mom."

"That's what I said."

Mya lifted her eyes heavenward. On her worst days, it behooved her to admit, with great lamentation, that it was still slightly, minutely, yet terrifyingly possible that she would become her mother.

Of course, that was her mother's dream. "Let's go to the kitchen. I think I can fix this."

And the thing was, Mya was sure she could.

Millicent Donahue owned a hair salon, aptly named Millie's Hair Salon. Despite the fact that the term had gone out of style in the eighties, she still called herself a beautician. For years the salon had been a bone of contention between mother and daughter. Eventually they'd called a truce of sorts. Now, Mya needn't feel obligated to have her hair trimmed at her mother's salon, and her mother needn't feel obligated to shop at Mya's store. Not that Mya carried red sweatshirts with glitter and sequins, anyway.

Mya pulled out a chair, her mother started clipping, Claire uncorked the wine and Suzette began unwrapping the trays of food she'd gotten from her favorite deli over on Market Street. The wind howled and rain pelted the windows. Sitting in her warm kitchen, surrounded by these quirky women who loved her, Mya relaxed. She liked her house. Built some eighty years ago of stone quarried from the area, it was a good house, Cape Cod in style, small and sturdy with a steep roof and a bay window overlooking the street. Oh, it wasn't on Keepers Island, and it was old and drafty, but it had character and was close enough to the Atlantic to feel like home.

"I thought Jeffrey was going to be here," Millicent said around the hair clip in her mouth.

"He had an emergency."

"An E.R. doctor," Suzette grumbled. "Do you have any idea how many women aspire to marry a doctor?"

"I didn't aspire to marry anyone."

"Go ahead. Rub it in."

Mya smiled into her chest.

"I still say it isn't fair," Suzette said.

"What isn't fair?" Millicent asked.

Pouring the wine, Claire said, "Don't mind Suzette, Ms. Donahue. She's just bitter because Jeffrey saw her naked first and still chose Mya."

"My daughter is a goddess."

Drolly, Mya said, "No goddess ever had this haircut."

"Rolf's an idiot."

For once, Mya wasn't even tempted to argue.

In seemingly no time at all, her mother stepped back and handed Mya a small mirror. Although still slightly shocking, evened up here and there, the tousled style looked pretty good on her, all things considered.

Her mother said, "You haven't had hair this short—"

Their gazes locked.

With the barest lift of one penciled-on eyebrow, Millicent said, "—in a long, long time."

Mya should have known she needn't have worried.

Her mother was the first to look away, and Mya was left feeling a dozen emotions, none of them pleasant. So what else was new?

Oblivious, Suzette said, "What do you say we move this party out to the dining room and away from any airborne hair?" Taking a small tray in either hand, she headed for the door, disrupting Jeffrey's three cats that had somehow wound up at Mya's place.

"What do you have there?" Millicent asked.

"There's crab dip with tofu and whole-wheat crackers, goat cheese and fruit and honey, and—" The door swung shut on the rest of the recitation.

Millie reached into the cabinet for the chips and into the refrigerator for the dip. "Forget the health food. I need all the preservatives I can get." When she was certain Suzette was out of hearing range, she lowered her raspy voice and said, "If that girl gets any perkier, I'm going to bite through my tongue." She followed Suzette to the dining room.

Mya's thoughts exactly. It was no wonder she worried.

It was quiet in the kitchen suddenly. Too quiet. Finding Claire watching her, Mya handed over the other tray.

Claire put it right back down again. "You're really going to do this, aren't you?"

"Serve red wine with cheese? I'm living dangerously."

Claire didn't pretend to be amused.

And Mya said, "Not you, too."

"I'll say my piece, and then forever hold it. You're going to get married."

"I thought you'd be happier for me."

"I am happy for you." She must have read Mya's expression, because she said, "This is my happy face."

Another time Mya might have smiled.

Claire forged ahead. "You don't find it at all unsettling that you accepted Jeffrey's marriage proposal because of something Dr. Phil said on national television? *Love is a decision.* Where does he get this stuff? Will I take a cruise or climb Mount Everest? Shall I fix green beans for supper, or corn? Should I flunk the kid I caught cheating today or call him in and talk to him? Those are decisions. Trust me, love is not a decision."

"You don't believe I love Jeffrey?"

"I think you're fond of Jeffrey, much the way you're fond of your new living-room rug. Jeffrey is a nice guy. In fact, there should be a law against anybody being that *nice*, Suzette notwithstanding."

"What's wrong with nice?"

Claire gaped. "You chew up nice people for breakfast and spit them out before lunch."

"How flattering."

"Come on, Mya. A woman like you hasn't remained single this long for lack of opportunities. Don't even try to tell me Jeffrey's marriage proposal was your first."

Mya floundered for a moment. "Now I really am flattered, because the truth is, I haven't had all that many marriage proposals." She prayed Claire didn't expect her to be more specific.

"That's because you almost never let a man close."

Relieved, Mya said, "Jeffrey is attentive, intelligent, ardent and imperturbable."

Claire fanned herself with one hand. "You're making me hot. Tell me something. Why is it that your every description of Jeffrey begins with a vowel?"

Leave it to a high-school English teacher to notice that.

The kitchen door opened, and Suzette stuck her head inside. "Did you talk to her?"

Mya threw up her hands. "You two planned this?" Looking at these women whose personalities were at opposite ends of the spectrum, she said, "Let's just suspend my personal belief for a moment. Let's say love isn't a decision, and the fact that Jeffrey makes me think, makes me feel special and safe, *and* he's a good kisser isn't enough reason to marry him. How does a woman decide who to marry?"

With a flourish, Suzette took a sheaf of papers from her oversize purse. "I put that question to my second graders this morning. Claire, did you ask your class?"

"That was an assignment gone wrong. Trust me, you don't want to hear the results."

Suzette nodded. "My students' answers were problematic, too."

Now Mya was curious. "What did they say?"

"Nobody believes in true love anymore. Not even eight-year-olds."

"Maybe they're too young to *make a decision*," Claire said.

New lease or not, Mya gave her the finger.

Waving as if at a bothersome insect, Suzette said, "I asked my students how they would decide who to marry. The smartest girl in the class said you wait until you're old, *at least twenty*, and you go on a date, and if you believe half his lies, you go on another, and at the end of the summer you get married."

Mya smiled.

Suzette didn't. "Her best friend said you don't decide. God does. You have to wait until you're grown up and see who you're stuck with. The boy who sits next to her stood up and declared that no age is a good age to get married. You got to be a fool to get married."

"Nine will get you ten he'll be sitting in the back of my class ten years from now," Claire said. "If he's still in school then."

"That's awfully judgmental!" Suzette admonished.

"You say judgmental, I say realistic. Potato, po-tah-to."

It was like watching a tennis match. Times like these, Mya understood why she'd started watching Dr. Phil's program every chance she had.

"Are you bringing more chips?" Millie called from the next room.

Suzette dashed toward the door with the bag of chips, practically tripping over one of Jeffrey's cats. When the door stopped swinging, Claire said, "And that's another thing, Mya. You're a dog person. You don't even like cats."

Mya scooped two of the oversize fur balls off the kitchen counter before they sampled the crab dip. Depositing them, none too ceremoniously, in the back room, she closed the door and brushed at the cat hair they'd left on her green silk blouse. "You have it all wrong. Those sneaky, obese, flea-ridden creatures don't like *me*."

"What's not to like?"

Back in control, Mya let that go.

Claire looked worried, but she said, "Listen. It sounds like Jeffrey's here. We'd better get out there and save him from Suzette."

Right behind her, Mya said, "You mean from my mother."

Oh, sure. Now Claire laughed.

"You're positive you don't want something to drink?" Mya held up the bottle of wine.

Jeffrey put it back on the coffee table where she'd gotten it. "Booze and E.R. duty don't mix."

The man was just about perfect, no doubt about it. "You're not hungry?" Mya asked. "Not even for apple slices dipped in honey?"

Everyone had gone, and Mya was trying to put things away. Uninterested in putting anything away, Jeff put his arms around her. "I'd rather have a different kind of honey."

Claire was right. Jeff was so nice he was corny. Corny wasn't all. Thirty-two years old, Jeffrey Anderson stood six feet three inches tall, had linebacker shoulders, a washboard stomach, hands and feet like a Labrador puppy *and the sex drive of a seventeen-year-old.* The thought burned through Mya's mind before sliding away to a place she didn't go anymore.

Nuzzling her neck, Jeff said, "I have to be back at the hospital in thirty-eight minutes. We can spend the next half hour doing anything you want, anywhere you want."

Now what kind of woman could complain about that? He knew all the moves, and she would have to be a fool to waste them. And yet she always had the feeling he was asking for permission. Jeff was a gentleman. There was nothing wrong with that. Still, sometimes she wished he would just take her, devour her, infuse her with passion and delight until she writhed in ecstasy.

He turned her gently into his arms and kissed her again. Holding her to him, molding and kneading until she groaned, he eased her backward toward the sofa, where they'd last made love. She'd had a crick in her neck for two days.

"I think what you have in mind is best suited to a bed, Doctor."

His face lit up as she reached for his hand. He'd lit up this way when he'd first laid eyes on her earlier tonight, too, although he still hadn't said anything about her hair. He would either say something nice, or he wouldn't say anything at all, of that she was certain. Jeff was a nice guy. Mya's relationship with him was the most calm and rational one in her life. Until recently, she and her mother had rarely missed an opportunity to argue. Claire was of the opinion that the Donahue women weren't happy unless they were miserable. Claire should talk. She could learn a great deal from *Dr. Phil*, if only she would tune in.

There was no reason in the world to be thinking about this, especially when a virile, nearly naked man was undressing her, caressing her, kissing her. Where was her blouse, anyway? Jeff peeled away her bra and covered her breasts with his big hands. Pleasure surged through her.

Mya was five-four-and-a-half, and at times Jeff seemed as big as a house. He was her safe place in the storm of life. She'd discovered it that night in the emergency room. It was the first time she'd set foot inside a hospital in years. She wouldn't have then if she'd had a choice. She'd managed to remain stoic through the harrowing drive to the hospital, Suzette whimpering in the seat next to her. And then she'd managed to get Suzette into a wheelchair and through the automatic doors. She'd given the night nurse all the pertinent information. After they'd wheeled Suzette away, and Mya was alone in the cold, austere hospital, panic had set in. She'd shaken with the effort to hold herself together. And there was Jeffrey coming off duty, bringing her a cup of steaming coffee and the offer of a broad shoulder to cry on.

Jeffrey Anderson was just about the nicest, kindest man she'd ever met, and she'd found herself wondering if she'd been holding the wrong kind of man at bay. He'd asked for her phone number. And she'd given it to him. She was sure he wouldn't call, even more sure she wouldn't go out with him if he did. She was wrong on both counts.

He'd called, and it had felt good to talk with him over dinner. And later, it had felt good to kiss him. After a few dates, it had felt good to make love with him. What was so wrong with feeling good? He didn't curl her toes. So what?

The wind howled and rain ran in sheets down her bedroom window. The room was shadowy and drafty. Goose bumps rose on her skin as he lowered her to the bed and eased down next to her. Heat emanated from him, drawing her closer.

The mattress shifted and their breaths mingled. She was tangling her legs with his when she glanced at the foot of the bed. Two cats sat nearby in the oblong patch of light spilling from the hall. A third had stopped in the doorway. All three were *watching*.

"Jeffrey. The cats."

He groaned when she stopped doing what she'd been doing and removed her hand, but he heaved himself away from her and gathered up his cats. "I swear you guys do this on purpose." Shooing them all into the hall, he closed the door. "Now, where were you?"

She laughed, and it almost sounded wicked. It had been a long time since she'd been wicked. He returned to her, and she enjoyed it so much she couldn't help laughing again. He kissed her, stroked her, caressed her, until a deep feeling of peace entered her being. She spoke his name on a whisper, and he came to her, the joining of man to woman pure and pleasurable. Those first delightful tremors were just beginning when one of the cats yowled in the hall. The other two took up the cry.

Feeling her stiffen, Jeff said, "Pretend we're in the jungle."

Mya laughed, and he smoothed one fingertip along her cheek, down the length of her neck, skimming the outer swell of her breast, her waist, until he found what he was after. He was an ardent lover, mindful of her needs, and vocal about his. And yet she was distracted. Who wouldn't be distracted with three cats yowling outside the closed bedroom door?

A memory came, unbidden. Hazy and as if from a great distance, she glimpsed for but a moment, two lovers too young to know what they were doing, and a passion so consuming nothing could have kept them from doing it. She stopped the thought, her mind suddenly blank, her body and soul empty.

"I love your hair."

Mya started. "What?"

"Your hair. I like it. Very sassy."

He'd waited until it was pitch-dark to tell her. But it made her smile, and it brought her to him once again.

She moaned softly.

"Do you like that?" he asked, his voice low.

"I think you should do it again, just so I can be sure."

This time he chuckled, but he acquiesced, and yes, she liked it. Maybe it wasn't ecstasy. Accepting the weight of him, and the warmth of him, it was enough.

Ecstasy was overrated, anyway.

"I love you," Jeff said. "I'll call you tomorrow." He sauntered to the foyer, bending to pet each cat on his way. He looked back at her from the door. Giving her a smile, he was gone, sated and content.

She envied him that contentment.

Where had that thought come from? Turning, she found all three cats staring at her, as if Jeff's leaving was somehow her fault. Jeff worked long hours. And when he wasn't working, he was at her place. It made sense that his cats were better off here.

"What? He has his house. I have mine."

The white cat jumped onto the back of the sofa. The yellow two continued to stare at her from the easy chair.

"You heard him. He'll call tomorrow." And then, because

she couldn't be cold or cruel, even if she wasn't a cat person, she added, "Don't worry, he'll be back."

No swish of their tails. No meows. No purring. Nothing.

Why anybody bothered talking to cats, she didn't know. Cinching the sash of her long silk robe, she padded to the kitchen. The moment she started the electric can opener, all three cats came running.

She doled out the bribe, and watched them enjoy it. The white one even let her pet him, and she had to admit, his fur was soft and warm. Leaving them to their late-night snack, she wandered through her little house. It was nearing the witching hour, and it had been an eventful day. Her hairstyle had been salvaged, she was learning to coexist with Jeff's cats, and she'd avoided a blowup with her mother. Maybe she'd finally grown up—perish the thought—but she was thirty-six.

She looked out the kitchen window. The rain had let up and the wind had died down. Dark, damp and cold, it was a good night to brood. It was what the old Mya would have done. What good had it ever done? What good would it do tonight?

She did an about-face. Instead of brooding, she was going to leave this mess for tomorrow and go to bed. She hadn't taken three steps when a knock sounded on her door. She paused at the lamp she'd just turned off. Her neighbors never stayed up this late. Jeff had a key, so it couldn't be him.

Maybe Claire or Suzette had returned for some reason. She doubted it was her mother.

The knock came again.

Turning the lamp back on, she went to the door and peered through the peephole. The room pitched, and one hand flew to her mouth.

A girl wearing faded blue jeans and no jacket stood on the porch. Mya felt frozen in time and in place, and yet she opened the door, a wild gust of wind hitting her in the face.

After looking Mya up and down, eyes the same brown as her own narrowed. "I would have knocked sooner but I was waiting for the Minute Man to leave." With a snide curl of her lip, the girl said, "Hey, Mom. Long time no see."

CHAPTER 2

Mya moved only enough to force a deep breath.

All these years she'd wondered what her child looked like. Here she was, technically no longer a child. Her pale blond hair was shorter than Mya's, even after today's fiasco. Brown eyes cold with fury, she was the spitting image of Mya at that age, anger, belligerence, bitterness and all.

"Don't tell me you're going to faint."

Still holding perfectly still, Mya said, "I've never fainted in my life."

"Lucky you."

Although she'd tried not to, sometimes Mya had imagined a mother-daughter reunion. Some of the scenarios had been tearful, others awkward. None had depicted a nineteen-year-old girl skinny enough to be blown away on the ocean wind, glaring at Mya with eyes as cold as stone.

Mya glanced at her watch. "It's after midnight."

"Yeah, so?"

"Happy birthday."

Elle Fletcher clamped her mouth shut. She didn't know what she'd expected, but it sure as hell wasn't the emotion burning her eyes and throat. Other than the funky hairstyle and the whisker burn on her neck, the woman looked pretty normal. It was disturbing, how much the brown eyes reminded Elle of her own, right down to the tears brimming in them.

The hell with that! This woman wanted to cry, let her. Elle wasn't about to do the same.

She'd been parked down the street long enough to see two women get in a four-by-four and drive away. Not long after, an older woman had climbed behind the wheel of a red boat on wheels and left, too. The man stayed the longest, which wasn't saying a lot, but he'd finally cleared out, too.

That left *her*.

Her name was Mya Donahue. She was single and thirty-six, and she owned this house as well as a clothing store called Brynn's over on Market Street. Some of the information had been in the file at the adoption agency. Most of it had required a little digging to uncover. The rest would have to come from Mya, herself, if Elle decided to continue. She didn't want to. She wanted to turn tail and run as far away as she could get.

It was as if Mya knew. Her expression still and serious, she took a backward step, and opened the door farther.

If she'd voiced the invitation, Elle wouldn't have taken it. As it was, she glanced over her shoulder, torn. The night was dark, the street empty except for her rusty Mazda.

She'd come this far. Might as well see if any of it had been worth it. Drawing herself up, she went in.

Not about to allow her relief to show when she closed the door against the damp and the cold, she glanced around the small room, taking in the eclectic mix of furniture and color. There was a throw over the back of the sofa, the usual magazines and junk mail on the end tables, a pair of shoes on the floor next to an assortment of feather toys. "You have a cat?"

"They're my fiancé's."

Elle snorted, then went and got caught looking at the open bag of potato chips and a plate of cheese. Her guard back up where it belonged, she glared at Mya, silently challenging her to make something of it.

"Would you like to sit down?"

Elle shook her head. And the woman, *her birth mother*— Elle welcomed back her anger—seemed to accept that.

"What's your name?"

"Eleanor. If you want me to answer, call me Elle."

"Hello, Elle. You're shivering."

"That's my problem. You gave up all rights to my problems when you signed on the dotted line, didn't you?"

Mya's smile held a touch of sadness. Glancing away, Elle felt a wretchedness of mind she hadn't planned to feel. Her stomach growled. Gritting her teeth, she would be damned if she would be embarrassed about being hungry.

"Could I get you something?"

"What? You wanna brew some sweetened tea and maybe make some toast for me?"

"And have you throw it in my face? Is that what you want to do?"

Élle hadn't expected that. It was almost as if Mya knew her, or worse, understood her. Impossible.

"I didn't come here to eat."

It must have taken a lot to refrain from asking why the hell she did come then. Elle stifled the thread of respect trying to worm past her defenses. Mya Donahue hadn't earned any respect. She was nothing to Elle, or almost nothing.

As nonchalantly as possible, Elle glanced out the window toward the street where her car sat, undisturbed. "I have to go." She could feel Mya watching her, could sense the questions she wanted to ask. "What?" Elle asked, and dammit, she couldn't keep her lip from curling snidely.

Mya shook her head. "Do what you have to do, but you're welcome to come back."

Elle took flight before she did something embarrassing, like sink to the sofa and rest her head for a minute, or worse, blurt out the reason she was here. She ran to her car and unlocked it. Mya didn't follow her or call to her. But she stood in the open door in the cold damp wind. The sight burned the backs of Elle's eyes.

Nobody said this would be easy, but the fact that it was

this hard still ticked her off. The anger was fuel, and she used it to get the hell out of there. She drove carefully, though, for it wasn't anger that had brought her to Maine. She was pretty sure Mya had picked up on that fact. Pulling into a parking space in the cheapest motel she'd found, Elle swallowed hard. When she was certain it was safe, she leaned over the backseat, unfastened the safety belt, and took the best thing she'd ever done into her arms. Ten-month-old Kaylie sighed in her sleep, comfortable and secure.

Her daughter's warmth and weight girded Elle's resolve and renewed her courage to do what she had to do. It was possible that all the courage in the world wouldn't be enough.

"Geez, Mya, long time no see."

Mya gasped at Claire's terminology. She didn't remember the drive to her friend's loft on the waterfront, but Claire had been waiting for her, so she must have called ahead. Vaguely, Mya recalled pulling on the clothes she'd worn all day. Even Claire might have been put off if Mya had shown up in her bathrobe.

Claire said no more until Mya came to a stop at the huge windows overlooking island-studded Casco Bay. "What's happened?"

Mya wasn't certain how to answer. She wasn't certain of anything. Had she come here to confide in Claire? Or did she need to see the lights dotting the ocean, the tanker on the horizon and the scattering of islands between here and there?

"Mya?"

She answered without turning. "I had a visitor after everyone else left tonight."

"Who?"

Again, Mya didn't know how to reply. Finally, she said, "My daughter."

Claire's silence finally drew her around. Poor Claire. She'd been awakened from a deep sleep. Still groggy, she blinked owlishly. "Your daughter?"

"I had a baby, Claire."

"So that's your secret. I always suspected you had one. Perhaps you should start at the beginning."

She started in the middle, but she reached the beginning quickly, ending with Elle's surprise visit tonight. "Nobody here knows about my past. Except my mother. And now you."

Normally Claire wore contacts, but after being awakened tonight, she'd donned a pair of glasses. A few years ago, Suzette had laser surgery to correct her vision, but not Claire. It wasn't because she hated hospitals, like Mya. Claire wasn't taking any chances with complications. Claire O'Brien was one of those people who looked at four ounces of liquid in an eight-ounce glass and saw the potential water stain on the table.

"Have you told Jeffrey?"

Jeffrey? Obviously Claire wasn't the only one who was dazed. "No."

"Are you worried about how he'll feel and what he'll say?"

How could she be worried when she hadn't given it any thought?

"Do you care what he thinks, Mya?"

Mya went from listless to ticked in under three seconds. Perhaps that had been Claire's intention. "What do you think?"

"I think that if you're going to marry him, you should tell him."

That *if* brought Mya up short.

"What's she like?" Claire asked, sinking into a nearby chair.

"She looks like me at that age, well, except for the piercings and tattoos."

"Sounds like half my students. How old is she?"

"She's nineteen today." Mya watched Claire's gaze go to her wild new hairstyle.

"What did she say?" There was nothing syrupy about Claire's voice. Steady and level, it invited trust. It always had.

Mya shrugged as she rose, inexplicably drawn to the window again. Or perhaps not so inexplicably. Unlike many of the islands in Casco Bay, Keepers Island was too far away to be visible from the mainland from this vantage point. It was out there as surely as she was standing here.

She hadn't set foot on the island in years, and yet she could picture it so clearly in her mind, the little harbor where the islanders docked their sailboats and skiffs and trawlers, the ice-cream shop and summerhouses near the beach, and the larger, weathered houses of the year-round residents farther inland, the square, brick school, and the sandy cove where she'd first made love.

Staring out across the bay, goose bumps rose on her arms. She had the strangest feeling someone was looking back at her. It was impossible, not to mention irrational. She got the hell away from that window just the same.

"Her name is Elle," Mya said, clasping her hands tightly together. "Short for Eleanor." It occurred to her that she didn't know the girl's last name.

"She didn't tell you why she came or what she wanted?" Mya scrubbed a hand over her face.

Claire said, "If you want me to stop playing twenty questions, just say the word. We can sit here quietly all night if you want."

And Mya was glad she'd come here tonight. She'd needed a dose of Claire's drollery and calm acceptance. "She stood in my living room a total of two minutes." And every second was permanently etched on her mind. "I don't think it's a matter of her wanting something. More than likely, it's something she needs."

"Money?"

Mya thought about the threadbare jeans, the missing coat and the rumble of Elle's stomach. "Something else. *What* remains to be seen."

"Then you believe she'll be back."

Mya found herself staring toward the window again. "She'll be back. I'd stake my life on it."

It was an hour past closing time, and Elle hadn't come.

Mya was disappointed, and when she was disappointed, she tended to get a little snippy. This time, the recipient had been a large-boned woman browsing through the rack of sale items. In her own words, she'd been "just looking." Translated, that meant she was killing time. Mya wanted her to kill time someplace else so she could go home and see if Elle was waiting there. Short of throwing the customer out, Mya had done everything she could think of to get rid of her. Turning out the lights hadn't been nice, but it had been effective. Finally, Mya locked the front door. Peering past the display in the window, she wouldn't blame the woman if she never returned. But at least she'd gone.

Thanks to the City of Portland's innovative revitalization plan, the waterfront district would be bustling with tourists in a few short months. Weekend traffic was always good, but at dusk on this Wednesday in mid-April, the brick-and-stone streets and sidewalks were practically empty. Only a handful of people strolled by. None of them had short blond hair, an obvious bad attitude and visible tattoos.

Elle wasn't coming. Mya had been so sure she would.

She hung up a garment that had fallen, but walked past the stacks of sweaters that needed to be refolded. Her boutique was a long, narrow space squeezed between a bookstore and a glass-and-art studio. What Brynn's lacked in square footage, it made up for in style. The walls were original brick, the hardwood floors worn smooth more than a century ago when this entire building had been used as a warehouse for the shipping industry.

Much of her summer merchandise had arrived this morning. Normally, Mya would have stayed late to catalog everything. Her mind would have been racing to decide how to best display the trendy skirts and summer sweaters and nautical jackets, the beaded pants and espadrilles, scarves and jewelry. Normally, she would have stayed until the wee hours of the morning, steaming away wrinkles and arranging everything on racks and shelves, in trunks and inside open drawers of antique armoires. Normally, she couldn't wait to get started. Today, she left everything in the cartons in the middle of the floor, switched on the night-lights, set the alarm and left, locking the back door behind her.

The alley was protected from the ocean wind. Taking a deep breath of air still warm from the sun, Mya reached into her pocket for her car keys. And stopped in her tracks.

Elle was leaning against her car.

A thrill ran through Mya as the girl sauntered toward her. Holding her explosion of pleasure to a small smile, Mya noticed that Elle positioned herself so that her car remained in plain sight, causing Mya to wonder if she was living out of it. The bottoms of her jeans were frayed, her plain black T-shirt tight. She looked less defiant, less confrontational. Her gaze was no less assessing.

Mya proceeded with caution. "There's an Italian bistro across the street, an English pub around the corner and oyster shacks and fabulous seafood places within walking distance in every direction."

She swore Elle looked tempted.

"And there's a little pizzeria past the next alley, and—"

"Pizza?"

"The best pizza in the universe." Hearing a noise, Mya looked overhead for seagulls. Seeing none, she said, "Care to grab a deluxe with me?"

"I can't." Elle was easing away.

Mya wanted to call her back, to beg.

Over her shoulder, Elle said, "Maybe one of those restaurants needs a waitress."

"Are you looking for a job?"

"I don't know yet."

"I could use a clerk at Brynn's."

"You're kidding, right?"

Elle was a dozen feet from her car when Mya called, "Do you hear a baby crying?"

"I've gotta go."

"Elle, wait." Mya practically ran to the car, only to freeze all over again, for the cries were coming from a baby in the backseat.

For a moment Elle looked as if she'd just been caught doing something bad. But her attitude returned, shoring up her chin. "She's mine."

Suzette claimed the most powerful sentences contained just two words. *She's mine* was proof enough for Mya. Since she didn't trust herself to speak, all she could do was watch as Elle put the seat ahead and squeezed into the back. Seconds later, she eased out again, the baby in her arms.

"Surprise."

Mya reeled, which was undoubtedly Elle's intention.

The baby stopped trying to drag her bonnet over her head, and stared at Mya as if the hat problem was her fault. Mya hadn't spent much time around babies, so she couldn't say how old the child was. Her cheeks were round, her eyes blue. What Mya could see of her wispy hair was blond. She wore pink overalls and tennis shoes, one lace trailing. The little Harley-Davidson T-shirt seemed at odds with the delicate bonnet.

"She's had an earache," Elle said.

Later, Mya would marvel at how in tune Elle was with

what Mya was thinking, but now she said the only thing that came into her mind. "She's beautiful. I sensed you were hiding something."

Elle made no comment, leaving Mya to wonder what else the girl was hiding.

"What's her name?"

"Kaylie. She's almost ten months old."

Hearing her name, the baby looked up at her mother, who smiled at her. Instantly, Kaylie's chubby little face spread into an adoring grin.

"Kaylie what?" Mya asked around the sudden lump in her throat.

"Kaylie Renee Fletcher. I was going to name her Harley, but in the end, I couldn't. Couldn't picture an old lady named Harley. I figure if she doesn't like Kaylie when she's thirty, she can shorten it to Kay."

The "old" reference wasn't lost on Mya. "And her middle name?"

"Renee was my mom's name. It's my middle name, too."

Mya absorbed every last implication, from the quiet reverence in Elle's voice, to her use of the past tense. "Where did you grow up?" she asked.

Elle's eyes narrowed.

And Mya said, "Yours isn't a Down Easterner's accent."

"My parents moved to Pennsylvania when I was about Kaylie's age." Suddenly, Elle didn't seem to know where to look.

The girl inspired a curious urgency in Mya, a sense that time was spinning too fast. She wanted to ask her a hundred questions about where Elle had been and what kind of life she'd had, but she settled for asking only one. "Are you going to stay in Portland for a while?"

"I'm thinking about it. It's not like we have anyplace better to be."

"Kaylie could come with us to grab that pizza."

"She already ate." With that, Elle returned the baby to the car seat. Before she was through, she loosened the ribbon beneath Kaylie's chin. Immediately, the baby stopped fussing and began the arduous task of trying to remove the bonnet.

Elle left without saying goodbye. After she drove away in her noisy little car, Mya got in her shiny, midsize model and drove away, too.

Time, she thought as she stopped at the light, was an amazing thing. Sometimes an hour seemed to last forever, and then one day you discovered that an entire lifetime has passed. Elle was young and still believed thirty was old. Mya had spent the last nineteen years trying *not* to remember how it felt to be that young.

Jeffrey was scribbling on a chart when Mya arrived at the hospital. He smiled when he saw her. It did little to relieve the knot in her stomach. Motioning to a small lounge, he held up five fingers. She knew from experience that although his intentions were good, he would be at least ten minutes, probably fifteen.

The staff lounge was deserted. Decorated in shades of purple and gray, the room was aesthetically pleasing enough, if one liked hospitals. They happened to terrify Mya.

Perhaps she should have waited for Jeffrey at his condo. Conveniently located a few blocks from the hospital, his place had high ceilings and tall windows that made the most of their southern exposure. For all the building's wonderful character, the furnishings were early bachelor pad. She'd told him that nobody had a water bed anymore. With a shrug, he'd given her free rein to change the decor as soon as she moved in. Mya wanted them to live in her house after the wedding.

One hurdle at a time.

Claire was right. People who were engaged needed to be honest with each other. She had to tell Jeff about Elle.

She paced, leafed through a magazine, then paced again. Her mind wandered, and she found herself wondering where the labor and delivery rooms were in this hospital. They'd been on the second floor in the hospital up in Brunswick, where she'd—

The sound of laughter drew Mya around. The young nurse entering the lounge stopped laughing when she saw Mya.

"Tammy," Jeffrey said behind her, "Would you mind using the other lounge?"

Although *Tammy* left, it was apparent to Mya that she did mind.

Jeffrey paused just inside the door, right after he smiled. And Mya wondered what he saw in her. He obviously had plenty of opportunities. Why her?

"Still trying to figure me out?" he asked. "I told you. Men are simple. Sex and supper pretty much covers our needs."

"So you say. Do you realize I've never seen you angry?"

"Why would I be angry? You're here. Life just got better."

"You're very smooth, Doctor." When he grinned, she was reminded of the first time she'd seen him in this very hospital. The man looked good in scrubs, no doubt about that. She wished she melted at the sight of him.

Where had that come from? What was wrong with her? She was afraid she knew the answer.

"You want to see smooth?" he asked. "Come here."

She remained where she was. "I have something to tell you."

He went to her and kissed her. "It must be important to bring you here."

"It is."

"If you don't want to keep my cats at your house, I can move them back to my place."

"And here I was getting used to all the cat hair."

"God, you're gorgeous."

"You always call me gorgeous when you're trying to get me out of my blouse."

"I like the way you think."

She grasped his wrist when he reached for her top button.

"I'm teasing, Mya. What is it?"

"Perhaps we should sit down."

He studied her in a manner that caused her to understand why he was so well liked and respected and appreciated in E.R. "In my experience," he said, "there are three things a woman might say when she looks at a man the way you're looking at me. *One*, she's married. *Two*, she's gay. *And C*, she was once a man."

Mya couldn't help smiling a little. "Prepare to add one more possibility."

She'd suggested they be seated, yet he was the one who drew her to a vinyl sofa on the other side of the room. "Okay," he said when he'd taken the adjacent chair. "What is it?"

She'd practiced her speech during the drive over. Unfortunately, there was no way to soften the bluntness of what she had to say. Forcing her gaze on his, she said, "I had a baby."

His eyes widened, but he didn't flinch.

"When I was seventeen. I held her once, and then handed her to the social worker." She kept her voice even, her memories locked up. "I never heard from her again."

He continued to watch her closely.

"Until last night."

"She called?" he asked.

"No. She came by."

"So she looked you up. That's common, isn't it?" Jeffrey said. "They're curious. Justifiably so."

Mya fought an unholy desire to stomp on his foot. "Elle doesn't strike me as the crous type."

"le?"

"Eenor. There's more." Mya tucked her short hair bhind her ears. She missed her long hair, missed the weight of it and the warmth of it. More stble now, she said, "She has a ten-month-old bby girl named Kalie. I know this must come as a shock."

For what seemed like foeer, the oly sound in the room was the ticing of the clock on the wall bhind her. Fnaly, Jeff spoke. "What's shocing is that all these months I've been sleeing with a granmoter."

Now, she did nudge him.

"Hoey, the sounds you make when we're making love give the word new meaning."

She jumped to her feet. And as he had dozens of times before, he went to her and put his arms around her. "This doesn't change the way I feel about you, if that's what you're worried about." He slid his hands down her back, drawing her against him. "You're beautiful. You're smart. You're sexy as hell. Something that happened to you when you were a kid doesn't change any of that."

"It wasn't something that happened to me. I wasn't run over by an 18-wheeler or struck by lightning. It was something I did, a portion of my life I lived."

"Potato, po-tah-to."

"Now you sound like Claire."

"That hurts. My parents want to meet you."

She blinked. "They do?"

"I think you'd better find out what Eleanor's after. She probably just wants to know her medical history, now that she has a kid of her own. No sense getting bent out of shape until we know what we're dealing with, right?"

Bent out of shape?

For some reason, Mya couldn't get comfortable in his arms. She couldn't find that safe place, that warm sense of being home. He kissed a path along her neck. Normally, she responded to the sensation. Tonight, she wondered what he would look like *bent out of shape* and thoroughly ticked off. She reminded herself of the anger-management classes she'd taken, and the self-help books she'd read. Jeffrey was sane and rational, and this was how sane and rational people dealt with life's issues. Sanely and rationally.

"Jeff." She stepped out of his arms. "Someone could come in."

He released a long sigh, but he followed her toward the door. "What are you going to do?"

Until that moment, she hadn't a clue. Bending down for

her purse and jacket, she said, "I'm going to pick up a pizza."
The statement was delivered in a tone of voice that encour-
aged him to go ahead and make something of it.

He didn't, of course.

As she left the building, Mya wondered what Dr. Phil
would say about the fact that she was disappointed. In the
pit of her stomach she knew it wasn't sane or rational.

Maybe she hadn't come so far after all.

CHAPTER 3

Elle entered Brynn's through the front door the following morning. Mya was busy with a customer who kept commenting on her hair. Elle didn't know what that was all about, but she hiked Kaylie higher on her hip and waited. Thankfully, she didn't have to wait long. Mya rang up the sale, placed the purchases in a lime-green bag, then followed the customer to the front of the store. The fact that the woman looked wealthy didn't keep her from staring openly at Elle.

The moment the door closed, Elle said, "The rumors will be flying now."

Mya's eyebrows rose a fraction, but her voice was level as she said, "I can handle rumors. How was the pizza?"

"I'm not a charity case. Is everyone who comes in here full of herself?"

Mya's gaze was direct, her pause palpable. "Evidently."

The woman didn't take much crap. To Elle's annoyance, she respected that. She didn't know why she was dishing it out in the first place. She'd been surprised when she'd heard the knock on her door last night. "Pizza delivery for Elle Fletcher."

She'd opened the door but not the chain, and saw a boy who was probably still in high school start to smile. Wearing a baseball cap and a jacket bearing the pizza store's logo, he held the flat box out to her.

"I didn't order any pizza."

He'd fumbled in his pocket for the order pad then checked the address. Pizza delivery guys were always nerds. It was probably in the job description.

"It's bought and paid for," he'd said. "My job was to deliver it." A nerd with a bad attitude, he put the pizza on the step and left without another word.

She may have been belligerent and too broke to give him a tip, but she wasn't stupid. She'd taken it inside. While Kaylie used a crust for a teething ring, Elle sank her teeth into a thick slice of lukewarm pizza loaded with cheese, mushrooms, onions and pepperoni. She'd wolfed down three pieces before she thought about the example she was setting. Hopefully, Kaylie was too little to pick up bad table manners. The thought seared the back of her mind, bringing a sense of dread and sadness she refused to give in to.

"The only reason it tastes so good is because I haven't sprung for pizza in a while," she'd told Kaylie as she started on her fourth slice. "That doesn't mean it's the best pizza in the universe."

Kaylie drooled solemnly from the middle of the bed. Elle had gone to sleep with a full stomach. And then she'd finished the pizza for breakfast while she fed Kaylie her oatmeal.

She knew she should thank Mya. Instead, she eased Kaylie out of reach of a rack of sunglasses and said, "What did you do? Follow me?"

"If you're asking how I knew where to have the pizza delivered, I called the nearby motels and asked to speak to you."

"I should sue them for breach of confidentiality. That's a big thing these days."

"Lawsuits or confidentiality?"

"You tell me." For some strange reason, Elle was glad Mya could hold her own with her. Not many people could. Elle didn't know why she was dishing it out in the first place. She looked Mya up and down. Her skirt had an uneven hem, her top a knit number with pink and green stripes. There were bangles on her wrists and dangles in her ears. Elle found herself looking at the diamond ring on Mya's left hand. "What do you think the Minute Man is going to do when he finds out about me?"

"His name is Jeffrey. And I told him last night."

Elle blinked, and Kaylie strained to get down. She'd been fussing a lot lately. Mya seemed to be having a hard time taking her eyes off her.

"Ever since she learned to crawl, it's all she wants to do. I haven't been letting her crawl around much in our motel room."

"How long have you two been on the road?"

"We left Pennsylvania a week ago, but we've pretty much been on our own since before she was born."

Kaylie was getting worked up. Elle tried moving her to her other hip, but it didn't help. When Kaylie got something in her head, there was no changing her mind.

Elle saw Mya reach her hand toward them, but it took a few seconds to notice the key held between her thumb and forefinger. "What's that for?"

"You can let her crawl on the floor at my house."

"Aren't you worried I'll make off with the good silver?"

Kaylie was crying in earnest now, so they practically had to yell.

"I don't believe you drove all the way to Maine to rip me off."

Their gazes locked.

It was the perfect opening, but Elle couldn't bring herself to take it, so instead she said, "What would we do all day?"

"Do whatever you want. Play with the cats."

"I don't like cats."

For some reason, that made Mya smile. It took everything Elle had to tear her gaze away.

Mya continued to hold out the key. Relying on instinct, Elle took it and turned quickly, only to stop. Kaylie quieted, and in a meek voice Elle barely recognized as her own, she said, "Thank you."

And then she got the hell out of there.

The bell had stopped jangling before Mya remembered to breathe. She had no idea what that had been about, and yet she'd won that round. The fact that Elle hadn't put up more of a fight made her uneasy.

Elle inspired a curious urgency in her. It was similar to the way she used to feel the last week before school started when she'd been a child, when the sun was still scorching and the days still felt endless, but she knew the end lurked like an alligator under the bed. Back then, she'd never wanted school to start, not because she didn't like school, but because she hated endings. She used to cram every summer experience into that last week, from ice-cream cones, to lobster bakes on the beach, to catching fireflies in Mason jars.

She felt that same sense of urgency now. She wanted to get to know Elle. She wanted to flip the Closed sign in the window and spend the day at home. With her daughter. She didn't know whether to be shocked about that or worried. Somehow she doubted Elle would appreciate being smothered. Mya knew the feeling. For years, she'd backed away whenever her mother tried to hover.

Oh, no. Her mother. Claire and Jeffrey knew about Elle. She had to tell her mom.

* * *

In Elle's words, the house was rocking.

Mya didn't remember the last time it had been this noisy in her living room. The television was on, Claire and Suzette were engaged in a heated debate over the president's foreign policy, Jeffrey was refereeing, and Elle was changing the baby.

"Mom," Mya said into the phone. "Would you listen?"

"What's all that noise?"

"There's something I need to tell you."

"What are all these cars doing in front of your place?" Millicent asked.

"You're on my street?"

"Are you having a party?"

Mya had to plug one ear in order to hear. "Mom, don't come inside yet."

"Just a sec. I need two hands to park."

"Mom, wait. Listen."

Static. Great, she'd laid the phone down.

"Mom?"

Silence.

"Mother!"

The line went dead mere seconds before Millicent burst into the house, smiling all around. "Why, it is a party." She beamed at Jeffrey, and didn't seem to notice that everyone except Kaylie had quieted. Talking to anyone who was listening, she said, "Who does Mya know who has a baby?"

Her gaze found Elle, and her mouth dropped open.

Suzette closed the door. And Claire caught the oversize red purse before it hit the floor.

Somebody turned down the television, and Millicent traipsed forward, stopping a few feet in front of Elle, who looked shy suddenly.

Mya said, "Mom, as I was trying to tell you—"

"It's you," Millicent said.

Looking from Elle to her mother, Mya said, "This is Elle Fletcher and Kaylie. Elle, this is—"

"I'm your grandma. I've been waiting a long time to meet you properly." Millicent's voice shook with emotion. "And this is Kaylie, you said? Hi, sweet thing!" Ducking down slightly in order to be at the baby's eye level, she said, "It looks like somebody's having a bad day."

Jeffrey said, "I checked her over. I think she's cutting teeth."

Millicent straightened again, patting Elle's arm. In a whisper loud enough to penetrate steel, she said, "Teething's a bitch, isn't it?"

She let Jeffrey take her coat. Speaking to Mya on the way to retrieve her purse from Claire, she said, "A little forewarning would have been nice."

The chaos resumed while Mya was still holding the phone.

* * *

"The last time I kissed a girl goodbye on the front porch, I was in the tenth grade."

Mya had to tip her head back in order to look into Jeff's eyes. "At least this brings back fond memories."

"Not that fond. Any idea how long Eleanor plans to stay with you?"

He called Elle by her full name. Not five minutes ago, Elle had referred to him as Minute Man, and Mya was pretty sure he'd overheard. Either he didn't mind, or he wasn't letting on. It was hard to tell with him.

Mya's mind was spinning. Claire and Suzette were two of the best friends Mya could ask for. Both had come over as soon as she'd called to tell them her daughter was here. Keeping the conversation lively, Suzette had gone off on one of her favorite tangents, insisting there was a reason all this was happening in Mya's life at precisely this time. Evidently, it all had to do with Mercury conjoining Uranus, and not one but two black holes. Or did she say Pluto was retrograde and the moon was in Taurus? Which didn't explain anything to Mya. She didn't even know why she was thinking about Suzette, except that Suzette had been even livelier than usual tonight, sharing a plethora of knowledge of everything trivial all evening.

"Did you know," she'd asked Jeffrey, "that rubber bands last longer when refrigerated?"

While poor Jeff was still struggling to find the relevance in that fascinating information, Elle had reached into her pocket and brought out a rubber band she'd found on the floor. Handing it to Suzette, she'd said, "Better put this in the fridge so we're prepared for the imminent shortage."

Suzette wasn't amused, but Claire, Millicent and Mya couldn't help laughing. Jeffrey had looked at them as if they'd lost their minds. Maybe they had. Or maybe the moon really was responsible.

"Mya?"

What? she thought, feeling irritable suddenly.

Oh. His question. "I get the feeling Elle isn't planning to stay in Maine for long," she said. "I'm surprised she accepted my invitation at all."

Jeff squeezed her hand. Although she knew he would have preferred a different scenario for his night off, he'd been a good sport, all things considered. He really was a nice guy. Loneliness twisted and turned inside her. There was no reason for this. The man who wanted to marry her was standing right here. Closing her eyes, she felt guilty and selfish, two of her least favorite emotions.

"Tired?" Jeff asked.

"I guess."

"It's been a rough few days. I'll call you tomorrow." He tucked his hands into his pockets. Instead of leaving, he transferred the contents of his right hand to hers. "My contribution to the cause."

Mya found herself staring at more rubber bands, and surprised herself by laughing. Watching him walk away, she thought that maybe, just maybe, everything would be all right.

The moment Mya stepped inside, three generations of Donahue females stared at her. Millicent was perched in the rocking chair, Kaylie on her lap. Elle sat cross-legged on the floor where she'd been trying to coax the white cat out of hiding.

Hanging up her jacket, Mya asked, "Any luck?"

Elle shrugged in a manner Mya was coming to recognize. "This cat's come the farthest. The other two haven't ventured out from under your bed since Kaylie discovered their tails before lunch. The Minute Man looked a little put out."

Mya didn't waste her breath telling Elle that all three cats had names, and so did Jeffrey. "He was just surprised, that's all."

The rocking chair creaked as Millicent offered Kaylie her bottle. "You're going to have to do a little pampering to keep him happy, Mya, if you know what I mean."

"There are greater tragedies than going without sex, Mom."

"For God's sakes, don't let him hear you say that," her mother said without looking up.

"Don't you know anything about men?" Elle asked.

It was so nice to see that her mother and daughter had bonded.

Everyone was relieved that Kaylie didn't have an ear infection. Unfortunately, she was still fussy. Mya felt a little like chewing glass, herself.

"There, there, sweet thing." Millicent patted the baby's back as she rose.

"She's not deaf, Mom."

"Now you're an expert?"

"I didn't say that."

"Here. You take her."

Before Mya could protest, her mother dumped the baby into her arms. Mya had no choice but to hold her.

"Relax," her mother said. "You're stiff as a board. Babies are like dogs. They sense when you're nervous."

Mya glanced at Elle. "You don't mind that comparison?"

Shrugging, Elle said, "It looks like Kaylie thinks you're doing okay."

Miraculously, it was true. Pink cheeked, her eyelashes matted from her tears, the baby stared solemnly up at Mya as if trying to figure out something important. But she didn't look particularly worried. Mya was nervous enough for both of them. "You know, kid," she said, "you're heavier than you look."

"How much did she weigh at birth?" Millicent asked.

"Six-and-a-half pounds. It seemed like a lot at the time. How much did I weigh?"

Millicent looked to Mya to answer.

In a quiet voice, Mya said, "You weighed six pounds, fourteen ounces." There was absolutely no reason for her throat to close up, and yet it did.

The room was silent. While everyone was trying to decide where to look, Kaylie figured out what it was she'd been pondering, and tried to stick her finger up Mya's nose.

She was quick. But Mya was quicker.

"Good dodge," Elle said. "She's had a thing for noses lately."

"When Mya was two, I had to take her to the emergency room because she put a button up her nose," Millicent said, very matter-of-fact. "I guess it's not surprising she's marrying a doctor. Isn't he as close to perfect as a man can get?"

Mya's diamond ring glinted beneath the lamplight. Another brittle silence ensued while she told herself there was nothing wrong with her diamond ring or with Jeffrey. Maybe that was the problem. Or maybe the flaw lay within her. Struggling with her uncertainty, she began to walk slowly around the room, the way she'd seen her mother do earlier. With a sigh, the baby rested her head on Mya's shoulder.

"Kaylie resembles you, Elle," Millicent said.

"Except for her eyes," Elle said. "They're blue like her father's."

Mya found her mother watching her. Something power-ful passed between their gazes. *Elle's* father had blue eyes, too.

A flash of grief ripped through Mya. Part of it was guilt for depriving her mom of her only grandchild, but that was far from all of it, for her mother wasn't the only one Mya's decision had deprived. At the time, she'd been so certain she was doing the right thing.

"Well looky there," Millicent said when Kaylie's eyes flut-tered. "I've heard it often skips a generation." There was rev-erence in her mother's voice.

"What does?" Mya asked cautiously.

"That connection. It's instinctive. She knows you all right. You two fit."

Mya was peering down at the baby, therefore she didn't see Elle's expression still and grow serious. Millicent saw it, and it brought a dull sense of foreboding. The girl was keep-ing secrets. And Millicent knew from experience that when girls Elle's age kept secrets, there was usually hell to pay.

Mya knocked softly on Elle's closed door.

A quiet "Yeah?" came from within.

Poking her head in, Mya whispered, "Is Kaylie asleep?"

Elle nodded. A dim lamp illuminated one corner of the small room. Elle had pushed the double bed against the wall. The baby slept on her tummy on the far side, a small bump beneath the blanket.

"Be prepared for my mother to arrive with a crib tomorrow. I told her to talk to you about it first. Did she?"

Elle shook her head, but didn't seem to know where to look. And Mya found that the earlier belligerence had been easier to deal with than this reticence. She would have preferred to have this conversation later, when Elle felt more comfortable here, but Millicent was convinced that the girl was hiding something, and insisted this couldn't wait until morning.

"Are you coming in or what?" So much for Elle's reticence.

"Won't Kaylie wake up?"

"Once she's out, she stays out." Elle sat near the headboard in baggy flannel bottoms and a stretchy tank top that bared a small tattoo of a musical note that seemed at odds with the barbed wire tattoo encircling her other arm. "I had a good mom," she blurted. "The best."

Perching carefully at the foot of the bed, Mya said, "Did she and your—do you have any brothers or sisters?"

Elle sat cross-legged, her elbows propped on the pillows she piled in her lap. "She said I was all she needed. Well, me and Dad."

Kaylie hummed in her sleep.

"My mom was an attorney," Elle said. "My dad still is, but she quit when they got me. Sometimes she helped him with wills and paperwork, but most of the time she cooked and planned trips and dinner parties and carpooled and took me to soccer practice and music lessons and friends' houses."

Mya could picture that. "What was she like?"

"She was very intelligent and tall and kind of ordinary. She played the piano, and she laughed a lot."

Mya didn't know what to respond to first, the sense that it was exactly the kind of life she'd wanted for her baby, or the puncture wound that giving her up had left in Mya's insides. "It sounds as if she took very good care of you."

"Too good." The sound Elle made had a lot in common with a snort. "She spoiled my dad and me rotten. After she died, laundry piled up and the cupboards went empty. Dad and I didn't have a clue what to do about it. He remarried a year later. I guess desperate situations call for desperate measures, huh?"

Mya studied Elle's features, one by one. She was extremely thin, her face pale in the dim light. Her short blond hair was tousled, her brown eyes expressive. "So you have a stepmother."

"You'd recognize her relatives from the movies. They wore pointy hats, kept flying monkeys for pets, and one of her sisters perished when a house fell on her somewhere above Kansas."

Mya bit her lip to keep from laughing. "Not a lot of love lost there, I take it."

"I *despise* my stepmother."

"Despising people comes naturally to the Donahue women."

They shared their first genuine smile. A moment later Elle looked away.

"She and my dad have two kids of their own now. He spends a lot of time at the office. I would, too, if I were him."

Why, Mya thought, *couldn't life ever be easy, or at least fair?* Since she knew firsthand that wishing was a worthless pastime, she prepared for the inevitable questions.

"When you and Jeffrey get married, it'll be your first time?" Elle asked.

Mya answered cautiously, for it wasn't the question she'd been expecting. "It will be the first marriage for both of us, yes."

Running her finger along the edge of the pillow, Elle said, "He's not bad-looking, if you like jocks. And he'll probably pull in good money."

The white cat pushed the door open with his head then sat near the wall, judiciously surveying the scene. Of the three cats, he was the friendliest. Although Elle hadn't admitted it, she enjoyed his company. She slid one hand along the bedspread, wiggling a finger. He took the bait, jumping onto the bed as if all four feet had springs. It took only a few sniffs to make an assessment and deem her trustworthy before he curled into a ball at her knees.

"Casper likes you," Mya said.

"Casper." Elle snorted, but she petted the overweight cat. "Don't you think it's weird for a man to have three cats?"

"They were strays." Mya couldn't help wondering if that was how Jeffrey saw her.

"He doesn't seem like your type."

Tucking her dressing gown around her legs, Mya said, "You're as bad as Claire. Jeff's made me see reason so many times. I don't ~~smoke anymore~~. I rarely swear. I haven't even given other drivers the finger in ages."

"So you're marrying him because he makes you see reason?"

"Of course that's not why I'm marrying him."

"Then you're madly in love with him?"

Mya wished it was easier to nod.

Elle looked over at Kaylie. "I thought I was in love with Kaylie's father, but he cleared out as soon as the wand turned blue. Good riddance."

"He sounds like a fool."

"Yeah," Elle said. "Your mother said the Donahue women don't make good choices when it comes to men."

Their gazes met, held.

"Is that what my birth father was?" Elle whispered. "A bad choice?"

Outside, a branch scraped against the siding. Somewhere in the house, a clock ticked. A few feet away, Kaylie made noises in her sleep. Elle didn't move a muscle, and looked as

f she could wait all night if she had to. Mya knew she'd
waited long enough.

They both had.

CHAPTER 4

"His name was Dean Laker." His name rolled off Mya's tongue as if it hadn't been nineteen years since every other word had been Dean.

"Was?" Elle whispered.

"Is. His name *is* Dean Laker." Time obscured many things, but it hadn't dulled her memory of him, tall and lanky, stubborn and proud, impatient with life but not with her, cocky and arrogant, except the day he'd gone to see her when it was all over. It wasn't the first time he'd told her to go to hell, but it was the first time she'd seen him cry.

"I met Dean when my mother and I moved to Keepers Island when I was nine. His was the first face I saw when I walked into that little classroom of strangers. He stuck his tongue out at me, and when I didn't flinch, he sat back, studying me closer, and I knew I'd passed some secret, unspoken test."

Elle stopped petting the cat, focusing completely on Mya. "If you knew his name, why did you leave the box blank on my birth certificate?"

Mya didn't even have to close her eyes to relive the moment when, sitting on the edge of the bed, pen in hand, she'd hesitated over that space on the form. Her mother had gone out for a smoke and probably another good cry, so Mya was alone in her hospital room. In an effort to make things easier for her, she'd been given a room away from the other mothers. Mya felt isolated and scared and, God, *she'd wished*—never mind what she'd wished. She'd grasped her right hand to stop the shaking, and had wound up staring at her left hand. Her ring finger was bare by then.

Nineteen years later, she sat in a quiet bedroom searching for words that still wouldn't come. "When I look back on my life, it's as if the decisions I made and the events that led to them are lined up like dominoes a moment before the first one topples. So many times I've wondered what might have happened if I'd done one thing differently. Just one. Any one. But that day, I left the box blank because I was seventeen and I'd gone through twenty-three hours of labor, and I'd just spoken with a social worker, and my mother had done almost nothing but cry and I refused to give in and cry again, too."

"You and Dean Laker, my birth father weren't still together then?" Elle asked.

Of everything she'd said, Mya was surprised Elle had chosen *that* to question. "Dean and I broke up three weeks before you were born."

"Does he still live around Maine somewhere?"

"Yes."

"Do you ever see him?"

"No."

"Never?"

"The last time I saw him was eight years ago when I went back to Keepers Island to attend his father's funeral."

Elle seemed to be putting everything Mya said to memory. "Did you talk to him that day?"

"With the whole town looking on?" Mya made an unbecoming sound. "He took his dad's death hard, and besides, he was surrounded by his family."

"So he had a wife and a couple of kids by then?"

Mya shook her head.

"He isn't married, either?"

"No."

"Are you sure?" Elle spoke more loudly than before, then glanced at Kaylie, who slept on.

Puzzled by the question, Mya said, "I'm sure, Elle. My mother would have told me."

"How would she know?"

"She goes back to visit friends every summer."

"But you don't?"

Again, Mya shook her head. Some things were just too painful.

After taking a moment to absorb that, Elle said, "What does he look like?"

She studied Elle, feature by feature. Her pupils were dilated in the semidarkness, so that only thin a ring of brown encircled them. The diamond stud in her nose looked real. Even at her young age, there was a slight furrow in her brow. Mya had been on the receiving end of the girl's attitude, and yet it was apparent that Elle hadn't had an easy life these past few years. The heaviness that so often lurked deep in Mya's chest moved front and center. "A few minutes ago," she said, "when you smiled, I caught a glimpse of him. His hair is dark, though, and his eyes are blue, like Kaylie's. His nose has a little bump right here." She pointed to a spot on her own nose.

"Did he break it in a bar fight or something?" Elle asked.

"He caught a kick ball in the face at recess when we were in the fifth grade. They called an honorary out, due to all the blood. It cost me my home run, and my team the game."

Elle's eyes widened with humor. "Did he blame you?"

The double meaning drained the smile out of both of them. Mya didn't even try to answer.

Interestingly, Elle didn't pursue it. "What does he do?"

"He's a builder. He got his start doing odd jobs like shoring up porches and cleaning gutters and pointing brick. Word spread, and before long he had orders from the summer people who wanted decks and family rooms, additions and new kitchens. His brother works with him now. To hear my mother tell it, they're extremely successful."

"He has a brother?"

The question gave Mya pause. "He has two. And five nephews."

"Then I have cousins, on that side at least. What about on the Donahue family tree?"

Mya shook her head, confused. "I'm an only child and so was my mother."

"Where is your father?"

"I have no idea. I've never met the man." When Elle looked at Kaylie again, Mya knew she was seeing a pattern.

Elle said, "Your mother told me she buried two husbands."

"And divorced another."

"She was married three times?" Elle asked, surprised.

"She gets lonely."

Elle's left eyebrow rose a fraction. "You just defended her."

"I'll be more careful in the future."

They both smiled, but instead of bringing a feeling of closeness, it brought an end to Elle's questions. The girl stretched and yawned. Taking the hint, Mya started for the door.

At the last minute, Elle said, "Mya?"

"Yes?" she asked without turning.

"What would you have named me?"

There was a sourness in the pit of Mya's stomach as she looked back at Elle. Swallowing the lump that had come out of nowhere, she said, "I would have called you Brynn."

Elle tried the name out on her tongue. "Like your store."

"Yes."

"Does anyone else know that?"

Mya's answer was a barely perceptible nod.

"Your mother?" Elle asked quietly.

"No."

"Your friends?" Before Mya shook her head again, Elle said, "You told *him*, didn't you? Dean Laker. My birth father knows."

"Yes, Dean knows. Good night, Elle." Somehow, Mya managed to leave Elle's room without stumbling.

Back in her own bedroom, she turned out the light and closed her eyes. But her eyes wouldn't stay closed. She thought about the day Elle was born. Whenever she recalled that period of her life, it was always with a sense of great physical and emotional pain. Her labor had hurt so bad she'd cried and begged just to let it be over. And when it *was* finally over, she'd felt so empty.

She'd gone on. And she and her mother had started over here on the mainland. Millicent had opened her hair salon and eventually Mya had opened Brynn's. She'd taken night classes and she'd made new friends. And the emptiness had gone away.

Liar.

She sat up in bed, too keyed up to sleep, too raw to read. Fisting her hands, she fought hard against tears she refused to let fall.

Her phone rang, and for once she welcomed the interruption. Masking her inner turmoil with calmness, she checked the caller ID before saying, "Hi, Mom."

"Did you talk to her?" Millicent Donahue had never believed in wasting precious sweet time on *hello*.

"Yes."

"Did she tell you anything?"

"I did most of the talking."

"And?"

Sighing, Mya settled back into her pillows. "It went well, all things considered."

"She didn't mention anything horrible? She wasn't abused or mistreated or anything like that?"

"No."

"What about Kaylie's father?"

"He took off before she was born. Elle can't stand her stepmother, but the couple that adopted her were good to her."

"What could it be, then?"

"Mom, did it ever occur to you that her arrival might just be the beginning of something good?"

"You didn't see her face. There's something she's not telling you, and it isn't something good, mark my words."

In the background, Mya heard a muffled, masculine voice say, "Stop fretting, Millie, and come back to bed."

"It sounds like you have company."

Evidently Millicent missed the sarcasm in Mya's voice, because she answered very matter-of-fact. "It's just Porter."

Mya recalled mention of that name, but she hadn't known he and her mother were sleeping together. Suzette had said it best a year ago when she'd complained that it wasn't fair that a sixty-year-old woman had sex more than they did. Mya massaged her forehead, for there were some things daughters weren't meant to imagine.

"Did she ask about Dean?" Millicent asked.

"Yes."

"At least you got that over with. Are you sure you're all right?"

"I'm sure."

"Because one of these days that airtight seal of yours is going to burst, you know."

"And it's all going to come exploding to the surface." Mother and daughter spoke together.

"Well, it is," Millicent said.

Mya sighed.

And her mother said, "It's a mother's prerogative to worry, you know. Porter, for heaven's sakes." But Millie twittered like a schoolgirl.

"Good night, Mom." Mya disconnected the call without waiting for her mother's reply.

Leaving the phone on the stand next to the bed, she tried to sleep. Every time she closed her eyes, she remembered those first minutes following her baby's birth. The nurse had held the infant, and Mya had tried so hard not to look. But

Elle had been crying, and Mya had looked. The baby had been unbelievably tiny, and so helpless, her skinny little arms and legs flailing. She'd stopped crying when they wrapped her in a blanket. And then Mya had started. She'd cried until they sedated her. After that she'd slept for twelve consecutive hours.

She supposed it was inevitable that her mind wandered to Dean next. She remembered him so clearly, cocky after their first kiss. And there he was a week later, grimacing as he cradled his swollen hand after defending her honor. Another time he'd chased her at the water's edge, catching her, playfully wrestling her to the ground. Lying on her back in the dark in her double bed, she could picture him laughing, but she couldn't remember the sound. Everyone had said they were too young. It hadn't mattered. She'd never loved anyone the way she'd loved him. She never wanted to again.

Listening to the sounds of her own house at midnight, Mya continued to toss and turn. In her mind, she saw Dean as he'd been two summers after their first kiss, naked from the waist up, the top closure of his jeans unfastened, his eyes hooded, his face full of intensity as he whispered, "God, Mya, I hope you're sure."

She'd laughed, and it had felt so powerful and so wonderfully wicked. "What would you do if I'm not?"

"Not this." He'd rolled her underneath him and covered her body with his.

And she'd whispered, "I'm sure."

She'd never been quite that sure of anything again.

She punched her pillow and tried to get comfortable. It was no use. Sitting up, she swung her feet over the side of the bed and padded toward the bathroom for a glass of water. She paused outside the spare room, listening. The door was closed and all was quiet. Reaching the bathroom still lost in thought, she opened the door. And let out a screech.

Elle uttered a crass word then jumped backward, sending a small plastic jar flying out of her hand and rolling across the floor.

Automatically, Mya bent over to retrieve it. It was a few seconds before she noticed the pills in Elle's palm. "What are those?"

The girl looked stunned. And then she glowered. "Looks like you caught me."

Still blinking against the sudden brightness, Mya said, "What are you doing?"

"What does it look like I'm doing?"

Mya stared, mute.

And Elle said, "I do drugs. What can I say?"

The brown vial in Mya's hand resembled a pharmacy bottle. Reading the label, she said, "What is this, Elle?"

"That's none of your business, is it? If you want me and Kaylie to clear out, say the word." No matter how hard she tried to cover it, there was panic in Elle's voice.

Mya placed the jar carefully on the counter. "I said you were welcome here, and I meant it. Are you going to tell me what's going on?"

"Who says anything's going on?"

A stare down ensued. Elle clamped her mouth shut, and Mya didn't know what to do about it. As she left the bathroom, she thought of her mother's foreboding. Elle was hiding something. That much was crystal clear.

"Hey, beautiful. You can't live without me, can you?"

Jeffrey snagged an arm around Mya's waist and had her on top of him in his big king-size bed before she could do more than gasp. "What time is it, anyway?" he asked.

"It's a little after eight."

He'd worked late last night, and probably hadn't had much more sleep than she had. Two thoughts managed to find their way through her foggy brain. How could anyone be rudely awakened from a deep sleep without being mad? She voiced the second thought out loud. "How on earth do you men sleep with those things?"

He moved beneath her like a mountain lion stretching in a patch of sunshine. "Want an anatomy lesson?"

"That isn't what you want to give me." But she smiled. "I'm sorry to bother you. But this couldn't wait."

"We're not talking about sex anymore, are we?"

"No."

"That's too bad. I mean it. I'm bereft."

Perhaps, but he was getting over it.

"What's wrong, Mya?"

"It's Elle."

"What did she do?" When Mya shot him a cold look, he had the grace to look sheepish. "Perhaps I should rephrase that."

Climbing out of bed, she retrieved her purse and removed the small piece of paper containing the word that had been on that medicine bottle.

"What's this?" he asked, sitting up.

"That's what I was hoping you could tell me."

He stared at the word while he scratched his chest. "It looks like the name of a pharmaceutical drug. Judging by the length of the word and the prefix and suffix, I'd say it's a very expensive pharmaceutical drug. Where did you get it?"

"I walked in on Elle while she was taking it."

He got out of bed, buck naked. The man didn't have a self-conscious cell in his body. Civilized enough to don a pair of tattered sweats before traipsing past two large windows, he strode out of his bedroom and into the room he used as a study. Mya followed, quietly watching as he took a heavy tome from a low shelf. Hefting the book onto his desk, he opened it, and ran his index finger down one page and then another. He checked the spelling on the paper Mya had given him, then leafed through several more pages.

"Here it is."

As he skimmed the data, a change came over him, and she knew he was putting on his physician persona. With dread, Mya asked, "What does it say?"

"Are you positive about the spelling?"

She nodded, for she'd memorized the word letter for letter.

"It's a chemotherapy drug, Mya, used primarily in the treatment of non-Hodgkin's lymphoma."

She felt a nauseating sinking of despair. "Cancer?"

"Of the lymph system. You *saw* Elle take these pills?"

"She took something from a bottle that had this name on the label. It might have been aspirin." Talk about grasping at straws.

"How did she act when you saw her?"

"As if she'd been caught doing something she didn't want me to see." Mya closed her eyes. Elle hadn't been taking aspirin. Of that, she was certain.

"Medicine has come a long way, Mya." Jeff closed the book and put it away. "Scientists and oncologists understand the way cancer cells behave, spread, metastasize and react better than they ever have. New strides are being made every day. There are better treatments, longer periods of remission."

While Jeff continued to say all the things doctors always said, Mya pictured Elle shivering on the front porch, and mad as hell for being there. That brought Mya up short. Why *had* Elle come to Maine?

"Jeff, I have to go."

She'd interrupted him in the middle of his bedside speech. Nonplussed, he grasped her cold hands and drew her to him, wrapping his arms around her back. The heat emanating from him should have warmed her. And yet she couldn't stand still in his embrace.

"Before you jump off the deep end, you need more information and it's time Eleanor gave it to you."

Jump off the deep end?

She bristled, but she held it inside and left his house. She was on a mission. And her next stop was the Portland Public Library at 5 Monument Square.

CHAPTER 5

It was sprinkling when Mya left the library. By the time she drove across town to her mother's hair salon, the sky was engaged in a full-blown temper tantrum.

Inside the salon, her mother was sweeping the floor around her only customer, an elderly woman named Agnes here for her weekly do. Millicent took one look at Mya's face, and put down the broom. "Something's wrong. What is it?"

While Agnes napped beneath a large aqua hair dryer, Mya stared at the papers clutched tightly in her hands. The top page was rain spattered, the ink running in places.

"Just come right out and say it. No need to sugarcoat it."

"Okay, Mom."

"I mean it. I can take the truth."

"That's good, because—"

"What do you have there?" Her mother pointed to the sheaf of papers.

"Research."

"What are you researching? For God's sakes, would you say something?"

Beyond any defensive reactions, Mya sighed and said, "This is information about non-Hodgkin's lymphoma."

"Non-Hodg—oh my God." Millie dropped heavily into a chair at another station, then listened as Mya explained what she'd seen the previous night, what she'd learned from Jeffrey and then what she'd discovered at the library.

"Does Jeffrey think Elle has cancer?" Millicent asked.

"What else could it be?"

Her mother rose shakily. Switching off the hair dryer, she woke her customer. "I can't finish you today, Agnes. We're having a family emergency and I must go see my granddaughter."

Poor Agnes blinked the sleep from her eyes. "Did you say granddaughter?"

"Yes."

"I didn't know you had a granddaughter."

"I do. I'll tell you about her another time. Right now you have to go."

"But I have curlers in my hair."

"Take them out in an hour. You can keep them or bring them back next time. I'll make it up to you. Where's your purse?" She located the patent leather bag and a spring jacket and ushered the woman out the front door, the plastic cape around her neck and pink curlers still in her hair.

Millicent's hand shook as she locked up. Turning in a circle, she said, "I remembered Agnes's purse but I left mine inside."

"I'll drive, Mom."

"Good idea." Their shoes splashed through a shallow puddle. "I'm a bit of a wreck. You can say it."

"You're doing fine."

"Darned right I am. I'm worried about you, though."

"Don't, Mom."

"I see the way you look at her."

Mya started her car and pulled into the sparse traffic.

"Aren't you going to ask how you look at her?"

"Mother." It was issued as a warning.

"You look at her the same way you looked at her the day you had her, like you'll die if you can't keep her."

"Mom, please."

"I know, I know. You've read accounts of real-life mother-child reunions, and much of the time, the situations aren't pretty. Maybe a lot of grown adopted children get their medical history and, curiosity satisfied, return to their families and proceed to go about the rest of their lives, and their birth mothers are left wanting more. But Elle's here, Mya. You can't close that off."

"I'm not closing it off."

"Sure you are," Millicent said in perfect time to the windshield wipers. "That's how you've dealt with losing her all these years."

"I didn't lose her. I gave her up."

"And you never talk about it."

"What good would talking about it have done?" But Mya's decision weighed heavily upon her. It always had.

Millicent sighed. "This weather is really getting on my nerves. Turn here," she said at the first stoplight. "The quicker we get to your house, the better. We'll get to the bottom of this faster if we present a united front."

Mya and her mother, a united front. Would wonders never cease?

Elle opened her eyes to a wall of legs, two of which were ensconced in red slacks and the other two showcased to the hilt beneath a pink skirt. Both sets belonged to slightly damp but formidable-looking Donahue women.

Millicent aimed the remote at the television where a DVD movie had been playing. "Jeffrey says those pills Mya saw you taking are chemotherapy. That true?"

Elle sat up. "That didn't take long."

"That isn't an answer, missy."

Looking up at Millicent, Elle got a glimpse of how Kaylie would be some day. It brought a swell of pain that had nothing to do with her illness.

Mya said, "Is Kaylie taking a nap?"

Elle nodded, then didn't know where to look. She wound up staring at the two orange cats curled up together in the overstuffed chair across the room. They always did that, leaving the white cat out. Cats weren't so different than humans. "My stepmother doesn't want her."

Both Millicent and Mya leaned forward in order to hear. "She doesn't want who?" Millicent said.

But Mya knew what she was talking about. "Your stepmother doesn't want Kaylie?"

Elle nodded. "Brunhilde says Kaylie's a bad seed. Like me."

Mya's eyes darkened with a dangerous expression. "The woman really is evil."

"I told you."

Lowering to the edge of the coffee table, Mya said, "She's wrong, you know. You're not a bad seed. And neither is your baby. You do know that, don't you?"

Elle had to fight the urge to hide from that probing gaze. "You saying you might want her?"

Millicent gasped.

Next to her, Mya said, "God, Elle."

It wasn't the response she'd hoped for, but then, when was the last time Elle's wishes had come true? Not the day her dad told her about her mom's accident. Not a year later when he'd remarried. Not when she'd told Cody her period was late. It sure as hell hadn't come true when she'd been waiting for the results of her blood test three months ago. Why should today be any different?

"I haven't decided to let you take her," she told Mya. "I barely know you, right? But if you're sure you don't want her, tell me now. I have things to do."

"Of course Mya wants her."

Elle and Mya both looked at Millicent. And then Millicent and Elle looked to Mya, who was blank and obviously shaken. Awkwardly, Elle cleared her throat. "I don't have a lot of choices."

Mya sat back, duly rebuffed.

"Eleanor Renee Fletcher," Millicent said. "What is going on?"

Millie sounded exactly the way Elle used to imagine a grandmother would sound. She told herself the drugs made her weak, and that was the reason for the sad yearning that kept her huddled on the sofa.

"I didn't get my strength back after I had Kaylie. We figured I was anemic, but just to be safe, my doctor ran some tests. When the results came back, they said I had lymphoma. I was terrified Kaylie had it, too, but she doesn't." She paused a moment to silently acknowledge that one of her wishes, the most important wish of all, *had* come true. "We thought the first regimen of chemo would be enough, but my remission didn't last long. I'm winding down after the second round. I still have my hair this time, so it's a pretty sure bet the second round hasn't been successful, either."

"What is your doctor doing about it?" Millicent asked.

Elle uncurled her legs and eased her feet to the floor. "If the cancer is still there, they'll try more chemo. I could go in and out of remission for years. Unfortunately, all that chemotherapy poses its own risk. If the cancer spreads, my only real hope will be a bone marrow transplant. It would be a long shot even if I had a sibling who was a match." Looking directly into Mya's eyes, she said, "Since there aren't any, my only other option would be to find a match through the national bone marrow registry. Finding a close enough match from a non-blood-related donor makes survival more like a crapshoot."

There were twin circles of pink on Mya's cheeks. The rest of her face had paled. "Does your family back in Pennsylvania know you're here?"

Elle said, "My poor dad. He's not happy about it, but I've gotta make sure Kaylie's taken care of." She looked at Mya. "You're not running. That must mean you're considering it. Don't you think you should talk it over with the Minute Man?"

In the ensuing silence, all three heard Kaylie wake from her morning nap. Elle started to rise. Gently, Mya placed her hand on the girl's knee. "I'll go."

Watching Mya disappear down the hall, Millie said,

"That girl never could sit still in times like these. I told her you were hiding something bad. I'd give anything to have been wrong. You probably noticed that she holds a lot in. One of these days the dam's going to break. I doubt it'll be pretty, but we'll get through it, the same way we'll get through this. Together."

Elle wished she was half as sure about that.

They could hear Mya and Kaylie in the other room. Millicent was quiet. Elle figured the old lady was entitled to her own thoughts.

"Elle?" she finally asked.

"Yeah?"

"Is your stepmother's name really Brunhilde?"

Elle glanced sideways in surprise. "It's Roberta."

Millicent turned her head slowly and said, "Girl, I like your style."

In a million years, Elle hadn't expected to smile today.

"Kaylie and I are going to bed. Tell Mya and Jeffrey goodnight, Kaylie."

Kaylie stared solemnly over Elle's shoulder.

"It's only nine o'clock," Mya said, launching herself from the couch. "You're welcome to sit with us after you put Kaylie to bed. We'll watch any movie you want. Or we could always talk. Or play a board game or cards."

Hoisting the baby higher onto her bony hip, Elle started

down the hall. Mya had little choice but to fall into step beside her.

"Kaylie took a short nap today," Elle said. "Besides, I figure you and the good doctor have a lot to talk about." Upon reaching the spare room, she lowered her voice even more. "You want him mellow, start with a BJ."

Mya shot Elle a look the girl didn't have the decency to stick around long enough to see.

Jeffrey was waiting patiently when she returned to the living room. Fingers laced behind his head, he smiled. "It's amazing how young they learn these days."

It was just her luck he'd heard.

"She's right, by the way," he said.

Mya tilted her head slightly, giving him a sardonic look. Accustomed to her sardonic looks, he said, "I take it Eleanor confirmed your suspicions."

She wanted to shout, "Her name is Elle!" But her painstakingly acquired good sense kept her still. Besides, Elle was as bad when it came to names as he was.

Mya had been rehearsing what she would say all day. The afternoon had gone by in a blur. She'd opened Brynn's just before lunchtime. Suzette and Claire had arrived after school, and for once, she'd welcomed Suzette's positive outlook. After checking her personal tides of the moon chart, Suzette had deemed tonight a good night to discuss serious issues.

Issues didn't come much more serious than this.

As so often happened, she found herself at the window. The porch light was on, illuminating the soggy yard and competing with the quarter moon. "I know why Elle came to Maine. You were right about the drugs. They're low-dose chemotherapy."

"I'm sorry, Mya."

"She came here to put her affairs in order."

"What affairs?"

"She's looking for someone to take Kaylie. In case..." She couldn't think it let alone say it out loud. Looking at Jeff, she said, "Me, to be exact."

Jeff sat back. And then he sat ahead. But he said nothing. Mya wasn't sure what she'd expected, if she'd expected anything, but she wasn't surprised by his shock. She was still reeling, herself.

"This is probably more than you bargained for when you proposed..." she paused, calculating. "A week ago." Had it really only been a week?

He patted the cushion next to him. When she didn't take him up on his invitation, he made a sound universal to men and joined her at the window. He asked a lot of questions about *Eleanor*'s condition and prognosis and treatment. Mya answered as best she could.

"Did you tell her you'll take the baby?" he asked when everything else had been said.

"I didn't tell her anything."

"Do you want to raise Kaylie?"

A suffocating sensation tightened her throat. What did she know about babies? Until tonight, she'd never so much as changed a diaper in her entire life.

"There isn't anyone else, Jeff."

For once, she couldn't tell what he was thinking, but she was certain of two things. She wouldn't try to talk him into anything. And she didn't think she could bear to lose Elle this time. "I'm going to be tested to be a potential bone marrow donor."

He took his time absorbing that. "You'll need someone to order the test."

"Can you?"

"I'll look into it." In a voice that had gone noticeably deeper, he said, "Lymphoma is a stubborn disease. The non-Hodgkin's form is downright conniving. This is going to be a tough time for you. It would be easier if you tried not to get too attached to Eleanor."

Something vicious unfurled inside her. A battle raged someplace between her head and the pit of her stomach. She felt like a character in an old alien movie, and a creature from outer space was clawing through her skin. She thought about the anger management classes she'd taken, and the self-help books she'd read. She doubted that even Dr. Phil would be able to tamp this monster down.

* * *

Mya transferred all the plastic toys and stuffed animals from her hands into a wicker basket next to the sofa. Jeffrey had left a while ago. Their kiss had been strained.

Practicing her deep-breathing exercises, she straightened magazines and took care of soda cans. *In through the nose, out through the mouth.* In the kitchen, she gave the cats a midnight snack, then put them in the back room for the night, breathing deeply all the while. *In through the nose. Out through the mouth.* Panic solidified her breath. Breathing deeply wasn't helping.

What was she going to do?

What could she do?

She was on her way past the spare room when she heard Kaylie jabbering in a language Millicent called baby babble. Mya paused in indecision. After the shock of the previous night, she opened the door cautiously and peeked in.

The lamp was on in the corner, and Elle lay on her side on the double bed, her eyes closed, her chest rising and falling evenly. Kaylie stood clutching the rails of her new crib like a miniature prisoner intent upon making a break for freedom.

"I thought babies were supposed to sleep all the time," Mya whispered.

Normally a serious baby, Kaylie up and grinned. She looked adorable in white cotton pajamas with a row of pink bunnies on the collar and cuffs. Mya couldn't resist moving closer. "What do you need?" she whispered.

Kaylie lifted her hands to Mya.

Suddenly, Mya couldn't even manage *shallow* breathing. Carefully, she grasped Kaylie beneath both arms, painstakingly lifting her from the crib. "If you had any sense at all you would be put off by my lack of efficiency."

Kaylie saw everything, and often wanted what she saw. For now, she seemed utterly content to rest her head on Mya's shoulder.

Mya inhaled the scent of baby shampoo and something as pure and indescribable as the scent of morning dew. A lingering sadness crowded into her chest, and with it, a persistent, haunting, clawing question. What had she missed?

Closing her eyes on an old sorrow, she rested her hand upon Kaylie's back. Spreading her fingers wide, she held the baby close. She swore Kaylie sighed. Emotion swelled, bringing the question again. Dear God, what had she missed?

Folding Kaylie's blanket over one arm, she eased away from the crib. Across the room, Elle shifted in her sleep, drawing their attention. Mya could only wonder what the baby was thinking as she studied her young mother's face. Mya noted the mussed blond hair and the shadow Elle's eyelashes cast on her pale cheeks. Her full mouth was soft in sleep, and completely lacked the usual smirk.

What had she missed?

Mya squeezed her eyes shut, aching, because she'd missed everything, every ordinary day, every milestone, every breath, every memory, every moment. The lack of it, of all of it, haunted her to the center of her soul.

"Da," Kaylie said, pointing a chubby finger at Elle.

"Not Da," Mya said softly. "Mama." It slipped out on a gentle breath, uncurling in the air like wisps of fog.

She said the word again, to herself this time. Reaching down tentatively with the tips of her fingers, she smoothed the hair off Elle's brow, her touch so light the girl didn't stir. She'd held Elle once, briefly. Only hours old, she'd been crying, and Mya had been terrified. That hadn't changed.

Mya's chest heaved, but it wasn't a monster that reared up after all. It was far more powerful and so strong it was as if something made of steel inside her was bending. And then, with a final, forceful heave, the steel broke, and emotion surged over her like a tidal wave, dousing her with something fierce, something instinctive, something protective. Something maternal.

Love.

A lone tear ran down her cheek. She loved her daughter. She always had.

"Da," Kaylie said.

For absolutely no reason at all, Mya chuckled. "We're going to have to work on your vocabulary," she whispered.

Kaylie smiled at her own cleverness, showing all seven of her teeth.

"For now, what do you say we go find a cat for you to terrorize? Better yet, how about a bottle?"

"Da," Kaylie said as Mya carried her from the room.

Elle waited until they left to open her eyes. She lay in the drowsy warmth of her bed for a long time, listening and thinking. And planning.

This was it. The moment Mya had feared.

It had been an emotionally charged week. She and her mother had come the moment Jeffrey called to say the results from Mya's bone-marrow compatibility test were back. Millicent waited in the outer lounge while Mya went to Jeff's office. The room was the size of a broom closet and smelled of latex and medicine. Mya felt the walls closing in on her as she read the test results.

There it was spelled out in black and white. It might as well have been Greek.

Jeffrey explained what it all meant, using terms she'd never heard, such as HLA haplotypes and phenotypes, genotypes and Locus A and B. One line contained Elle's information, one Mya's. The two were poles apart.

The excruciating wait was over. Mya didn't match. She wasn't even close.

"But Elle looks so much like me. Everyone says so."

"The intricate components that make up bone marrow have little to do with hair color," he said, his voice quiet, calm, compassionate.

She wanted to crush the paper into a ball and fling it against the wall. She wanted to rail, to rant, to stomp her feet and shake her fists. And all she could do was stand there, blank and shaken, fighting for self-control.

Elle's adoptive father had called several times this past week. His concern for Elle was palpable. Sadly, he wasn't a close enough match, either. That wasn't surprising since he wasn't blood related. But Mya was!

"What now?" she implored.

Jeffrey came around from the other side of his cluttered desk. He reached for her hand, saying nothing at first. When he finally spoke, his voice was filled with compassion. "I know how difficult this is for you, sweetheart."

That monster inside her reared up again, because he *didn't* know. No one did.

"This isn't fair," she said, rigidly holding her tears in check.

"No, it isn't."

"I can't lose her again."

He didn't say that she might not have a choice, but it hung in the air between them. It seemed like a long time before either of them continued, and then they did so simultaneously.

"Jeffrey, you—"

"Mya, I—"

They stared at each other.

"Yes?" she asked.

"I suppose Eleanor will be returning to Pennsylvania now."

He'd just come off a twelve-hour shift, and Mya tried to give him the benefit of the doubt. "And do what?"

"And continue her treatment at home with her family."

"What am I?" She realized her tone of voice hadn't been nice. She didn't have it in her to care.

"Mya, I'm not the enemy here. You don't have to open Brynn's for another hour. Let's get out of here."

She wound up staring at him.

He continued speaking in soothing tones. "You're worried, sad and upset. We don't even know what Eleanor's condition is for sure, let alone her prognosis. She could live for years. Hopefully longer. Everything doesn't have to change."

Staring at him, she wondered how he could not see that everything had already changed. Suddenly, she knew exactly what she had to do. She slipped her engagement ring over her knuckle.

"Mya, what are you doing?"

She shook her head.

"You win," he said. "We can take Kaylie. If the need arises."

She blinked, refocusing on Jeff. His hair had been cut recently. He looked urban and professional, not to mention drop-dead gorgeous.

"I didn't know you wanted children. But we probably would have had a couple of kids eventually anyway, right?" he said. Obviously he'd been perplexed about having a ready-made family, justifiably so. And yet he'd sanely and rationally agreed to one. "It would be nice if we knew Kaylie's father wasn't a drug addict."

"This isn't about Kaylie!" Everyone in the surrounding offices probably heard that.

She'd surprised them both, and yet it was all so clear suddenly. The relationship had been destined to fail from the beginning. Jeffrey was intelligent and kind and would undoubtedly make some woman a wonderful husband. But not her. He wasn't her type. He was too sane, too rational, too nice, at least for her.

She finished removing her ring.

"Don't do this, Mya. I love you. No other woman has ever excited me the way you do."

"I'm not the right woman for you."

He grasped both her hands. "We're good together, you and I."

He looked so earnest just then, that she smiled, albeit

sadly. "The person you've known these past six months isn't really me. Believe me, you wouldn't like the real Mya Donahue."

He had little choice but to take the expensive, though uninspiring diamond ring.

"Besides," she said, "I hate hospitals. What was I thinking?"

"That you loved me?" There was a long, brittle silence.

With a dawning look of realization, he said, "Oh, no. I know that look. And I know what you're thinking. You love me but you're not in love with me, right?"

She shook her head.

And he said, "That's my best breakup line."

"It's a good one."

A look of innate sadness entered his eyes. If she'd been in his shoes, she would have been spitting mad, more proof that they were completely wrong for each other. Not that she needed more proof.

"I believe you have more experience at this sort of thing, Jeff. The last time I broke an engagement was nineteen years ago. Has the protocol changed? Never mind. I think I should be going."

"That last engagement. Was it to Eleanor's father?"

"Yes. And her name is Elle!" More shaken than she cared to admit, she walked to the door.

"I'll be here if you change your mind, Mya."

"No you won't. I give Tammy or one of the other night nurses two shifts, and they'll have you snapped up."

She left him with his ring, and whether he realized it yet or not, with his pride.

Millicent stood as soon as Mya entered the outer waiting area. "Well?"

Mya shook her head.

"Oh, no. I was so sure you'd match." The bout of scarlet fever Millie had lived through when she'd been a girl ruled her out as a potential donor. "What did Jeffrey say?"

Mya didn't reply until they'd reached the elevators. "What could he say?" She pressed the down button. If she'd been thinking, she would have used her right hand.

"Where's your diamond engagement ring?"

The three other women waiting for the elevator looked at Mya's bare hand as she said, "I believe Jeff put it in his pocket."

"Mya, what are you doing?"

The doors slid open. The three strangers got in. Before following them, Mya said, "I've already done it."

"You're under a lot of stress. You're sad and worried. This isn't a good time to be making life-altering decisions."

The elevator started to move. Feeling several pairs of eyes on her, Mya said, "That's the only time people make life-altering decisions, Mom."

"That explains why so many of them turn out badly."

The remainder of their descent was steeped in silence. That silence followed them through the lobby. Out in the parking lot, the sun shone gloriously, the air a balmy seventy-five degrees. It was warm for April in Maine. Everyone knew it could turn around and snow tomorrow out of spite. There was nothing spiteful in the breeze, or in the scent it carried. It was the scent of the ocean, and of homesickness.

"You're going to do it, aren't you?" Millicent said.

Mya stared straight ahead.

"You're going to call Dean."

"I'm going to do better than that, Mom."

She was going to Keepers Island to see him. And her mind was made up.

CHAPTER 6

Dean Laker spread the large blueprints out on his makeshift workstation. When the wind whipped up a corner of the top page, he slammed a brick down on one edge, then groped his shirt pocket for the cigarettes he hadn't smoked in ten years.

Stinking April wind, anyway.

April.

He scowled. April showers, April wind. *April fool.*

From the corner of his eye, he saw his foreman, who also happened to be his brother Grady speak to their newest employee. Great. Grady was ambling this way.

Stopping directly in Dean's line of vision, Grady removed his Red Sox cap, ran a hand through his hair, then replaced the cap precisely where it had been. "Next time you decide to give one of the guys a good reaming, run it by me first."

The least Grady could do was *pretend* to show a little respect and maybe attempt to hide his open disapproval. "Last I looked," Dean said, holding the rustling print down with both hands, "I owned this company."

"Last I looked, Jeremy was doing a good job."

Dean folded the blueprint to the next page. This project was an intricate building restoration that incorporated an open-beamed addition and included a major renovation of the rest of the house. It was exactly the type of work Laker Construction was known for, a reputation he'd worked damn hard to build. "Jeremy's hungover."

"He turned twenty-one yesterday," Grady said. "What? Now you don't remember how it felt to be young?"

Dean scowled again, because truth be told, he couldn't think of anything else today.

But Grady was on a roll. That was the problem with employing family. They didn't know when to shut up.

"The kid wasn't late for work. So he's moving a little slow. I'll keep him off a ladder and work him into the ground and he'll think twice before doing it again. Good help's hard to find, Dean."

"You're telling me?"

"Why don't you tell me? What's going on?"

Dean took out his calculator and refigured the truss system for the addition. "Who says anything's going on?"

"I do. You're ornery as sin from time to time, but you're rarely unfair."

Dean recalled the look on that poor kid's face. Oh, hell, he was going to have to apologize. And Dean Laker was even worse at asking for forgiveness than he was at asking for permission.

His brother squared off opposite him, hands on his tool belt, his back to the Atlantic. "April's almost over, Dean."

Dean tensed. That didn't mean he had to admit how close Grady was to a nerve and to the truth.

"You've been acting strange ever since you got back from lunch at Mom's. What did she say that set you off?"

"Leave it, Grady."

A change came over his brother. No longer looking at Dean, the younger Laker stared at a place over Dean's left shoulder. His quietly spoken "You've got company, bro," was completely unnecessary, because five seconds earlier the air had become so charged with electricity it raised the hair on Dean's arms. He knew without turning what he would find. Or who.

He turned anyway, doing a slow one-eighty. His mother had heard right. Mya Donahue was here on Keepers Island.

"You okay?" Grady asked quietly.

Since any answer was pointless, Dean said, "I'll make it right with Jeremy."

"You do that. Hey, Mya."

"Hello, Grady." Her gaze didn't leave Dean's face for long.

Dean knew, because his didn't leave hers at all. Evidently, Grady noticed, too. He took the blueprints from Dean and made noises about going to see a man about a sawhorse. On a good day, Dean would have told him it was a lame joke. But Dean wasn't having a good day.

Mya didn't look real happy, either. The incessant wind dragged at her short blond hair. It had been long the last time he'd seen her four or five years ago. Who was he kidding? The last time she'd been to the island was four and a half years ago, exactly. Before that, it had been three years. She came for funerals and weddings. She'd never bothered to look him up, and that was fine with Dean. It was better that way, because looking at her brought out feelings he wasn't proud of, and memories better left in the past.

Why couldn't Mya Donahue be like other women whose bodies thickened and whose complexions grew ruddy over time? Her clothes looked soft, trendy, upscale. Her face was thinner than he remembered, her brown eyes dark and appraising. As if realizing she'd been caught staring, her chin came up, her shoulders back.

Why the hell that rankled, he didn't know, but he said, "It looks like you're still pissed off at the world."

For an instant, her glance sharpened, but she kept her voice quiet as she said, "I've narrowed the field down to an even thousand. What about you?"

"I'm only pissed at you." He cringed a little inside, for he couldn't have proven that to the twenty-one-year-old kid he'd laid into earlier.

Mya stood six feet away, breathing between parted lips.

Potential rejoinders flashed through her mind at breakneck speed. And yet she didn't know what to say. Dean didn't seem terribly surprised to see her. Ticked and slightly put out, but not surprised. Which meant word was out. She'd expected as much, for she hadn't been the only passenger on the ferry to Keepers Island. The handful of islanders who'd accompanied her on the three-mile jaunt out to sea hadn't joined her on the upper deck. She was thankful for that, for small talk would have been beyond her capabilities today. Still, the fact that she was here would have been too great a discovery to keep to themselves. And when had anyone on the island kept anything to themselves? Mya wasn't certain who'd told Dean, but he'd been duly warned that she was here. She wished there was an easy way to tell him the rest.

Either the years had been good to him, or the ravages of time were apparent only on the inside. Unless he'd changed, it was more than likely the latter, for as a kid he'd internalized everything, his thoughts, his dreams, his emotions.

Today he wore his dark hair shorter, his faded jeans a little looser, his emotions every bit as hidden from view. He'd always reminded her of a geyser, calm until the steam started rolling. He'd been furious when she'd flung his engagement ring at him the day she'd told him once and for all that she was placing their baby for adoption. For the life of her, she hadn't known of a decent alternative. He hadn't seen it that way. She wasn't naive enough to believe he'd gotten over it. After all, he was the only person she knew who held a grudge longer than she did.

She sighed anyway. "Nineteen years is a long time, Dean."

His eyes narrowed, as blue and changeable as the Atlantic behind him. Before he blurted something he would regret and she would react to, she said, "Would you care to go someplace and maybe grab a cup of coffee?"

Although he didn't shake his head, she knew what his answer would be. He raised his voice in order to be heard over the scream of a power saw. "Just say whatever you came to say. As you can see, I have things to do."

A thin chill hung on the edge of his words, and yet she felt her ears heating. She wanted to tell him to forget it, among other things. She spun around to retrace her steps down the hill, only to stop in her tracks. This wasn't about her. It wasn't even about Dean.

Facing him again, she said, "All right. I'll say what I came to say, if you're willing to listen, that is."

His nod barely qualified as a nod at all, his stance strong and rigid. In that moment she saw him with such clarity, and knew he was bracing for a storm.

It took some of the storm out of her. "I was wondering if you would like to meet your daughter."

Braced or not, he staggered as if he'd taken a two-by-four to the backs of the knees.

"She's staying with me at my house for the time being. The next ferry to Portland leaves in an hour. If you care to hear more, I'll be at the dock until then." There was nothing she could do about the quaver in her voice as she added, "She needs us, Dean. You know I wouldn't be here otherwise."

Dean stood there blank and obviously shaken, and watched her walk away.

"What the hell do you mean she needs us?"

Mya hadn't taken fifteen steps. She knew, because she'd counted.

Inhaling a fortifying breath, she looked around for a place to sit. She hadn't brought her car over from the mainland, and had asked someone at the ferry dock where she might find Dean. The man had pointed her in this direction. Half an hour later she'd spotted Dean's blue-and-yellow Laker Construction sign from the harbor, and had walked up the hill.

Jagged rocks and cliffs and countless bays and inlets made up the rugged coastline of Maine. The shoreline of Keepers Island was much the same. The summer people would be arriving in five or six weeks. Then, the slip would be full of sailboats with colorful sails and motorboats of all sizes. For now, the locals still had the island to themselves.

They called this Coopers Hill, for it overlooked Coopers Harbor, and was the second-highest point on the island.

Most of the houses here were large and expensive and belonged to the summer people. She understood the allure, for the view was breathtaking. Unfortunately, she saw no place to seek shelter from the strong ocean breeze.

Still slightly winded from the uphill climb, she led the way to a park-style picnic table on a grassy knoll away from the screech of power tools and curious onlookers. When Dean was seated, she folded her hands on the table in front of her and tried not to fidget. As kids, she and Dean had come together with fierce and unbridled enthusiasm and not an ounce of shyness. Neither of them had grown shy over the years, therefore it wasn't reticence that made them both feel awkward today.

"I'm listening," he prodded.

Calling on the insight she'd garnered from all the self-help books she'd read, she tamped down her temper and said, "She knocked on my front door just after midnight on the eve of her birthday."

"Out of the blue?" he asked.

Mya nodded.

"What did she say?"

"Something like, 'Hey Mom, long time no see.'" Staring beyond Dean at the waves in the distance, Mya said, "Her name is Eleanor, but she prefers Elle."

"What is she—" His voice had been deep, and deepened even more when he began again, speaking their daughter's name for the first time. "What is Elle like?"

"She looks like me and acts like both of us."

He stared at her, absorbing the implications.

And Mya said, "Our mothers would say we deserve that, wouldn't they?"

In another lifetime, they would have smiled.

"She has more than one *visible* tattoo, a smart mouth, and before she ditched her semifinals last month, she was earning a four point at Penn State."

"She's not attending college in Maine?" he asked.

"The couple that adopted her moved to Pennsylvania when Elle was a baby."

Mya wondered if Dean was thinking what she was thinking—that all those times over the years, when she'd glimpsed a child the age their child would have been and had wondered if she might be theirs, had been for nothing, for Elle hadn't been in Maine in eighteen years.

"Her adoptive mother died when Elle was ten. I've spoken to her adoptive father. He seems like a decent man. Evidently there's a stepmother in the picture, with all the cliché ramifications. Since she's been a full-time student until recently, Elle still qualifies for her adoptive father's health insurance."

"What does health insurance have to do with anything?"

Mya was doing this badly. Trying again, she said, "A week ago I walked in on her while she was taking pills. It's the reason she came to Maine, why she looked me up. The pills are chemotherapy."

He made it halfway to his feet, then sat heavily again.

Feeling ill-equipped to explain, Mya simply said, "She has non-Hodgkin's lymphoma."

"She's dying?"

"No!" Waves broke far below, reminding her of an old saying about voices whispering in the desert and yelling near the ocean. Suddenly, Mya didn't have it in her to yell anymore today. "If her cancer spreads from her lymph system, a bone marrow transplant will most likely be necessary. My bone marrow doesn't match, but I'm not going to let her die." She'd issued the words like a decree, daring him to make something of it.

In the awkward silence that followed, they both stood. Hooking the strap of her purse over her shoulder, she said, "There's one more thing you should know."

She supposed she couldn't blame him for watching her the way a wary fisherman watched a tidal wave.

"Elle didn't come to Maine by herself. She brought her nine-and-a-half-month-old baby, Kaylie." Mya removed a business card from her purse and handed it to him. His expression told her nothing of what he was thinking as he read the name on the front. *Brynn's.* It was the name they'd planned to give their baby, if it was a girl. Instead, she'd been named by someone else.

He flipped the card over with deft fingers, scanning the back where Mya had written her home address and phone number. "Elle wants to meet you, Dean. Are you busy tonight?"

He shook his head.

"Stop over about seven. She and Kaylie will be waiting."

Needing suddenly to escape his probing gaze, she started along the path toward the harbor below.

"And what about you, Mya?"

His voice stopped her in her tracks, and held her there.

"Will you be there, too?" he asked.

Glancing over her shoulder, she gave him a nod that might have meant everything or nothing, then walked away.

"You almost made it an entire minute that time, Mya," Elle said.

"Very funny."

It was after seven on every clock in the house. The interminable day dragged on.

Elle sat cross-legged on the floor opposite Kaylie, who banged a wooden spoon lustily on an upside-down spaghetti pot. While Mya had been paying Dean a visit on the island, Elle had spoken with her doctors in Pennsylvania, who had arranged for her to have her blood tested at Portland Memorial. It meant more waiting, more worrying and a lot more praying. Mya paced, wondering how people did this.

"Bottom line," Elle said, tying Kaylie's shoe. "Do you think he'll show?"

Mya and her mother exchanged a meaningful look.

And Mya said, "He'll be here."

Millie seconded it with a firm nod. "The ferry's always late when the ocean's rough."

Needing something to do, Mya fed Casper. Jeffrey had taken the orange cats back to his place, along with the rest of his things. Upon learning that Elle and Kaylie had grown attached to the white one, he'd left it behind for them. Silently, Mya had listed all the reasons it hadn't worked out between them. He was too tall, too young, too sexy, too nice. Especially too nice. He was too calm, too understanding, too patient. He was a doctor, and she hated hospitals. And she'd known, watching him walk away, that none of it would have mattered if she'd loved him. She didn't know why she couldn't love him. Maybe Claire had been right. Maybe love wasn't a decision.

Mya only knew that if it was, that kind of love wasn't enough for her.

A knock sounded on the front door, freezing everyone in place, even Kaylie. Millicent recovered first. "I'll get that," she said, smoothing her shaking hands down her red slacks. "In about a minute, the awkward first round will be over and done with once and for all."

She went to answer the door.

CHAPTER 7

Dean stood on Mya's front porch, more nervous than a thirty-six-year-old man in his right mind ought to be. When had he ever been in his right mind where Mya Donahue was concerned?

True to his word, he'd apologized to his youngest carpenter, then surprised everybody by giving them the rest of the day off, with pay. After explaining to his brother the reason behind Mya's visit, he'd left Grady to tell the rest of the family. Dean had had more pressing things to do. He'd arrived at the ferry docks half an hour early. As if that wait hadn't been grueling enough, he'd been tempted to show Pete Jackson, the ferry captain where the gas was.

At least he didn't have to wait long for his knock on Mya's door to be answered. But it was Millicent, not Mya, who threw the door open.

"Dean Laker, if you aren't a sight for sore eyes."

"You're not so bad yourself. Hi, Millie." But his gaze went to the slip of a girl standing a few paces behind her.

If he hadn't seen Mya earlier that very day, he would have believed time had stood still. A dozen emotions, none of them pleasant, had been scrambling for attention ever since Mya's visit. The moment he laid eyes on Elle, that changed, and there was only awe.

He entered without waiting for an invitation. Transferring the gifts from his arms to Millicent's, he smiled at the girl. She was slender. Too slender? She was pale, but not overly so. Please God, he thought. She wore no makeup that he could see, no jewelry except a toe ring and a simple sterling band on her middle finger.

Bypassing a formal introduction, he took both her hands in his. "You're beautiful."

Light blond hair brushed her forehead, framing her eyes, which darkened expressively. "At least that's original. Everyone else says I'm the picture of Mya at my age."

She tugged at her hands, and too soon he had to release them.

"Although I have to admit," she continued, glancing away, "this morning when I stubbed my toe and was hopping around cussing, she said I reminded her of you."

His next grin came a little easier, but only until he followed the movement he caught out of the corner of his eye. Mya entered the room, holding the baby on her hip. The sight of it cut off his air.

"There's Kaylie now," Millicent said a little too loudly. "I'm assuming these gifts are for her?"

"Some are for Elle, too," he said.

Elle did the honors, unwrapping a soft, silky stuffed doll and a picture book for Kaylie, and a simple charm on a silver chain for herself. Next came two baseball caps, one in a size medium, one small enough to fit the baby.

Dean said, "Lakers are Red Sox fans from way back."

He wasn't at all sure what she would say, or if she would accept her status as a Laker. She looked at him as if studying him, feature by feature, then handed the doll to him, indicating that he should present it to Kaylie.

At five feet eleven, he towered over all these females, but as he took that doll with him across the room, he knew it wasn't his height that made him feel like a gangly teenager. It certainly wasn't the baby.

He spoke quietly to her, holding the doll toward her. She looked at it, then at Dean, then hid her face in Mya's neck. God, she was adorable. Her brief flirtation with shyness didn't last long. Unable to contain her curiosity, she studied him solemnly, much the way Elle had. Her eyes were blue, her cheeks pudgy, her wispy blond hair adorably flyaway. He must have passed the test, because she grinned at him, then held out both hands.

Surprised, he took her, lifting her easily into his arms. He didn't know whether it was her toothy grin that did it, or the slight weight of her as he settled her comfortably on one arm. But he was a goner.

Elle said, "You know your way around babies."

In the awkward silence that followed, he met Mya's gaze. It required effort to move it elsewhere. "I practiced on my brothers' kids."

"Mya said I have cousins."

"Five in all," he said.

"No shit?"

Elle ducked her head, and Dean realized he'd just witnessed another brief flirtation with shyness. But her outburst broke the ice.

"Believe me," he said, "My mother and two sisters-in-law share your dismay."

Before anyone knew how it had happened, they were all seated in Mya's living room. Kaylie sat utterly still on Dean's lap, the doll on the floor. She peered up at Dean, transfixed as he talked about his family on Keepers Island.

"Grady and Gretchen have two boys, Michael and Greg. Reed and Sylvia have three, Cole, Brad, and their youngest, Dougie. Their mothers are always telling them to wash their hands and put down the toilet seat, not that they ever listen. Sylvia claims they have selective hearing, like their fathers. The dogs like it, though."

"Dogs?" Elle asked.

"As many dogs as kids. All males, too. Their houses are zoos, but thanks to the boys, the dogs never go thirsty."

Millie made a face as his meaning sank in, but Elle laughed out loud.

Mya watched the exchange quietly.

Dean Laker looked good on her couch. That shouldn't have surprised her, for he'd always looked good anywhere. But he'd grown up. No longer an adolescent boy, his voice was deeper, his hands steadier, his chin stronger, his gaze more direct. Not that he directed it at her. His attention was trained on Elle. Mya not only understood his fascination and preoccupation with the girl, she shared it. It was difficult not to think about what might have been.

The phone rang. When Millie went to answer it, Dean said, "The family wants to meet you, Elle."

"Then you already told them about me?" Elle asked.

He nodded. "They've all waited a long time."

Mya tensed as Dean's gaze met hers. Maybe he'd meant it as a personal affront. Maybe not. But that was how it felt to her.

Millie returned almost instantly, handing Elle the phone. "It's for you."

Rising slowly, Elle said, "Is it my dad?"

Mya couldn't have been the only one that heard the wistful hope in her voice. Sparing a glance at Dean, Millicent said, "She said she's your little sister."

Kaylie started to fuss, and Elle paused in indecision. Huffing slightly, Millie reached for the baby. "Would you like your diaper changed, young lady? And then a bottle?"

Suddenly Mya and Dean were alone.

Poor Dean. Clearly, his nose was out of joint, and Mya couldn't even blame him.

"Dean, I—"

"Let's keep this about Elle, shall we?" He jerked to his feet. "I think I'll get some air."

Donning a jacket, she followed him onto her front porch. Dean stood near the top step, facing the street. The evening was quiet at dusk, crocuses and daffodils blooming along either side of the sidewalk, their colors muted in the fading twilight.

Mya hugged her arms close and said, "It's been an emotional day for Elle. It's only natural that she wants, maybe even needs, to speak with her, er, other father."

Seeing his shoulders stiffen, she chastised herself, wondering how else she might rub salt in the wound. "I think keeping this about Elle is a good idea." She reached out, instinctively finding his hand. "The important thing is she's here. I know she's glad you came tonight."

He looked at her, an emotion she couldn't name hiding in the backs of his eyes. He almost smiled, until he remembered why he didn't. He drew his hand away, and she knew that in her haste to reassure him, she'd gone too far. The animosity was back between them, and there was nothing she could do about it.

So what else was new?

* * *

"Trevor wet the bed again. And Bubbles died."

Elle dropped tiredly onto the bed in the room she shared with Kaylie. "The new Bubbles?" she asked her little sister.

"Mama says he was just sleeping." Lauren made a scoffing sound into the phone.

The girl didn't sound nine.

"Goldfish don't have long life spans, Lauren."

"'Specially not mine." She sounded genuinely sad. "Elle? When are you cing home?"

Home. The word reaed iside le. That house in Haburg hadn't felt like home since the day Brhide moved in. Elle loved her dad, and Laren and Trevor, too. She didn't know where she fit in, though. She thought about Milie and Dean and Mya. She didn't hear anyvoices coing from Mya's liing room, and wodered if her dad, she grmaced, her birth fther—grmacing again, she fnally dcided to think of him as Dean—had left. Ealier, she'd told Mya she'd talked to her dotor back in Pensyvnia. But she hadn't told her he'd given her the rsults of her last blood test. Elle was scared. Shewanted her mom, her real mom, the mom that had raised her util she was a litle older than Laren was now.

Larenwanted to know when she was coing home. Feeing holow inside, Elle had an important decision to make. She really needed to talk to her dad.

"I don't know what I'm going to do," Elle said.

And Lauren sighed on the other end of the line. There were almost ten years between them, and yet the sisters had always gotten along well. Much to Brunhilde's chagrin. She was always saying Lauren was exactly like her. Fortunately for Lauren, it wasn't true. Elle had always thought the girl was a lot like their father. Elle wondered who *she* was like, not outwardly, but deep inside where she kept everything private. Who did she take after there?

"Did I tell you I have a cat?" Elle asked.

"A cat! Lucky!"

"Yeah, lucky me." Her voice sounded odd suddenly in her own ears, for lucky wasn't a word she would have used to describe herself or her life, her new cat notwithstanding. She still couldn't believe she had a cat. It was hard to find fault with Jeffrey, that was for sure. She wondered if Mya was going to regret ending it with him. Then she thought about how tense things were between Mya and Dean.

Maybe she shouldn't have come to Maine. But what else could she have done?

"Elle? Are you still there or what?"

"I'm here. Actually, the cat's name is Casper, you know, like the ghost, because of his white coat."

"I thought you liked dogs."

"It's a long story, but Casper thinks he's a dog."

"Mom says Trevor can have a dog when he stops wetting

the bed. Why should I have to wait for him to stop acting like a baby? He's such a pain."

"He'd be easier to hate if he wasn't so darned cute and nice, wouldn't he?"

"Yeah."

Elle was pretty sure six-year-old Trevor was going to need therapy after Brunhilde was finished with him. "Hey, Lauren? Could I talk to Daddy?"

Elle heard a voice in the background. And then Lauren said, "I'm talking to Elle, Mama."

There was a series of clunks, followed by static, and then the voice in Elle's ear changed. "How are you, Elle?"

Great. Brunhilde was all Elle needed. "I'm okay."

"What do you need?"

Now there was a question. Obviously, the woman thought Elle had called, not vice versa. Far be it from Elle to set the record straight, for doing so would gain poor Lauren a lecture. "Is Dad home, Roberta?"

"As a matter of fact, he isn't. May I take a message?"

Elle had known her stepmother to behave more cordially to telemarketers. Of course, telemarketers weren't the enemy. "Tell him I said hello, okay?"

"I'll see that he gets the message."

The line was disconnected.

Elle lowered the phone, lost in thought. It looked as if she was going to have to make her decision on her own.

* * *

Millie was rocking Kaylie in the living room when Elle ventured from the spare room. Whispering, the eldest Donahue said, "I'm hungry for pizza. If you order, I'll pay."

"Where are Dean and Mya?"

Millicent motioned to the porch.

Elle went outside just as Dean and Mya were coming in. All three paused. Cuting off their entrance, Elle closed the door and said, "Millie wants me to order a pizza. What do you want on it?"

"Anything except anchovies." Mya reached into her pocket.

Dean reached into his. "I'll get it," he said.

"It's my home, Dean."

"Yeah, well, she's my kid, too."

Elle looked up, one finger over the send button on Mya's cell phone. "Millie said she'll spring for it. It's *just* pizza. I'm starting to see why you two didn't get married."

Both adults looked stricken. Mya was the first to look away. And Elle knew she'd scraped a nerve. It made her curious about why they hadn't married.

"Is Kaylie sleeping?" Dean finally asked.

"Almost. Millie's rocking her."

"I should be going. The last ferry leaves at eight-thirty, and it's a long swim if I miss it."

Mya's smile looked forced, causing Elle to wonder what

she'd interrupted. She figured her own expression was more in the *oh brother* category. More awkwardness followed, and Elle wondered if she should forget it, forget everything, just let it all go. But then she thought of Kaylie, and the conversation she'd had with her doctor earlier.

Dean said, "I really have to go, Elle."

She knew he wanted to touch her, maybe give her a hug. She was too numb inside for that, so she said, "Yeah. It's a little cold for that swim. Thanks for the gifts. Kaylie likes her doll."

Looking at her long and hard, he took the hint and went down the steps without touching her. He was on the bottom step when she called, "When?"

Dean and Mya looked at her. Both were strangers to Elle in many ways. Hell, in most ways. And yet there was something about each of them that felt strangely familiar. It was the way they looked at her as if she was something precious. It put a lump in her throat, but it also made her feel weird, as if she was being disloyal to her family. She hated to admit it, but she was scared. She wished...

What did she wish? That her mom wouldn't have died? And her dad wouldn't have remarried? That Cody still loved her? That she didn't have cancer?

Yes! She wished all those things. Every one of them was a waste of time and energy, and she had little of either to spare. She had Kaylie. She had today. And she was here.

Those were her *givens*. Everything else was a *maybe*. She'd always hated *maybes*.

Regardless of what she liked, disliked or otherwise, she had options to consider, difficult decisions to make. She didn't know why she slid her hands into her back pockets, but the moment she felt the baseball cap, it hit her.

With shaking fingers, she touched the bill of the cap. Dean had said Lakers were Red Sox fans. Was that what she was? A Laker?

It was time she found out.

Holding Dean's gaze, she said, "You mentioned that the rest of the Lakers want to meet Kaylie and me."

He nodded.

"When?" she repeated.

The pupils of his eyes dilated in the fading twilight, but he looked pleased as he said, "Sunday. One o'clock?"

So soon?

But she'd made her decision, and there was no turning back. "Where?"

"At my brother Reed's place."

"Does he live on the island, too?"

Dean nodded. "Mya knows the way." He looked directly at Mya. "Reed, Sylvia and the boys live in the old McCaffrey place near the cove. The family extended the invitation to you, too."

Elle and Mya stared after him as he climbed behind the

wheel of a dusty four-by-four and drove away. "He's not exactly a conversationalist, is he?"

Mya shook her head, for it was true. Dean was a man of few words. But what he said, he meant. Still, she'd received more enthusiastic invitations from the dentist.

A gust of wind dragged at the lapels of her jacket. Drawing the edges together, she thought about Dean's visit tonight, and then she thought about his invitation.

All the Lakers, all at once, all under one roof. Why not just get out the whip and the horsehair shirt?

Until today, she could count on one hand the times she'd been to Keepers Island these past nineteen years. Just as Elle's conception had changed the course of Mya's life nearly twenty years ago, her recent arrival in Maine was changing it again. It was forcing her to face serious issues she'd buried a long time ago.

Seeing Dean again reminded Mya of how intense he could be, how dark and brooding, and how dangerous that combination had been to the rebellious girl she'd been. The hold he'd had on her all those years ago was strong. She happened to know the hold she'd had on him was equally so.

That was then.

Sunday was two days away. And Mya knew darn well that wild horses couldn't keep her away any longer.

CHAPTER 8

The first thing Mya noticed when Dean opened his brother's door on Sunday was the aroma of fresh-baked bread and steaming seafood. The second was noise. It exploded upon them. High-pitched voices of boys engaged in raucous roughhousing blended with laughter and what sounded suspiciously like space lasers and explosions and someone yelling for the boys to stop. Dogs growled and barked playfully. Someone yelled for them to stop, too.

The ferry from Portland had left right on schedule. Casco Bay had been calm, and even though Mya, Elle and Kaylie had arrived on the island a little early, Dean had been waiting for them at the harbor. Dean had installed a car seat for Kaylie in the backseat, and Elle sat beside her. That left the front passenger seat for Mya. Dean pointed out landmarks to Elle. Mya had watched out the window as the familiar sights went by. Nerves had clamored in the pit of her stomach all the way.

Elle seemed more quiet than nervous. Stepping over a pair of small, muddy tennis shoes and a partially chewed rawhide dog bone, she said, "It sounds like all hell's breaking loose in there."

Dean held the door. "Around here all hell breaks loose on a regular basis."

The four of them entered a big country kitchen and mayhem. A little boy was playing tug-of-war with a large brown dog. The dog was winning. Two other boys were facing a computer screen. Joysticks in their hands, they rooted for their spaceships and shouted at each other with all the rowdy vehemence of true competitors.

Up to her elbows in sudsy water, a red-haired woman called, "Dougie, let Buster have his blanket. Michael and Brad, turn off that computer game. Brad, where's your mom? Who's on guard duty at the front door? Reed, would you hurry up with those table leaves?"

The game of tug-of-war continued as if she hadn't spoken. So did the computer game. Another woman came bustling into the room, a heavy-looking table leaf in her hands. "Grady and Greg are keeping an eye out for them in the living room."

"It takes two?"

"You know Grady and—" The brown-haired woman stopped abruptly at the sight of Mya, Elle, Kaylie and Dean.

Coming to a stop a hairbreadth behind her, Reed Laker said, "Dean! Well, hell's bells. Come on in, everybody!"

A hush fell.

The boys at the computer looked over their shoulders.

The smaller child and the dog both dropped the tattered blanket. The poor redhead turned, suds dripping from her hands. Looking pained, she rushed toward them, drying her hands on a kitchen towel as she came. She smiled at Elle, Kaylie and Mya, and spoke sternly to her brother-in-law. "Dean Laker, I gave you strict instructions to use the front door."

Dean had the grace to look sheepish. "The front door's for company."

And then holy hell broke loose all over again.

"Hey, Uncle Dean. I'm whipping the pants off Brad."

"Are not."

"Am so."

"You wish."

"Wishes are for wusses."

The dark-haired woman handed the table leaf to her husband. "What a lovely first impression." But she managed to smile.

Mya relaxed a little at that smile.

The computer game was turned off, the dogs let outside, quick introductions made. The kids were presented en masse: Cole, Greg, Dougie, Michael and Brad. Mya already knew Reed and Grady, of course, and through the years her mother had kept her apprised of the additions to the Laker family. Grady's wife's name was Gretchen, Reed's, Sylvia. When it came to the kids, it was hard to tell who was who.

"The food's hot and the boys are hungry," Sylvia said. "None of us will have a moment's peace until we feed them. Boys, wash up. Use the soap. On your hands, not on the towel. Don't think I won't check." It was her house, and she was in charge. She handed Mya a heaping platter and directed Elle to put Kaylie in a well-used old wooden high chair.

As Mya took her assigned chair in the dining room next to Elle, she stole her first glance at the gray-haired woman sitting at the far corner of the table. Dean's mother smiled serenely. When everyone was seated, she bowed her head. "Welcome Mya, Elle and Kaylie. Now, let's all say grace."

One of the kids whispered, "Grace."

And two others giggled.

Reed led a short prayer. And then the eating commenced.

Two minutes into the meal, Mya realized that her unease had evaporated. Who had time to be uneasy? There were serving bowls to be passed and names to try to get straight and conversations to keep up with.

Elle sat next to her quietly, as if taking it all in. Mya wondered what the girl was thinking. The Laker boys ranged in age from about four to sixteen. All but the middle one had dark hair. There was no question that one was Sylvia's child. Kaylie barely moved in the unfamiliar high chair, a spoon clutched in one chubby fist, a crust of bread in the other. Eyes round, she seemed mesmerized by the sheer commotion.

"How do you like Maine so far?" Reed asked Elle, buttering his roll.

Before she could answer, Grady said, "If I were you, I'd reserve judgment until July when the weather turns truly glorious."

And one of the boys said, "Maine weather is famously harsh. What's the matter? Don't you like lobster?"

Suddenly, all eyes were trained on Elle, who dubiously eyed the heaping platter of steaming lobster in front of her. "I've never had it."

"Never?"

An older brother nudged him.

"There isn't a lot of fresh seafood in northwestern Pennsylvania," Elle explained.

"Oh, yeah."

With a wink, Reed said, "You're in for a treat. Isn't that right, guys?"

The second oldest of the boys—Mya was pretty sure his name was Greg—said, "Dad says the task of eating lobster isn't clean or easy. If you don't end up with butter all over your face and shirt—"

"You're not doing it right," two others said in unison.

Not about to be coerced into anything, Elle said, "I heard the poor creatures scream when they're dropped into a boiling pot."

There was a momentary hush. And then the red-haired boy said, "That's a myth."

"They don't have vocal cords."

"The sound is air leaving the body cavity in a rush."

"No sh—kidding?" Elle asked.

Everyone grinned, the kids especially.

"Dig in. You hafta use your hands." The oldest demonstrated, pulling the claws off and cracking one open.

All five kids got in on the instructions. The hard-shelled body and tail were snapped apart, and the pale flesh dug out. The boys used their fingers. At their urging, Elle did the same. There was more laughter, and second helpings of everything, and a glass of milk spilled. Gretchen wiped it up as if it was an everyday occurrence, engaging the others at the table in conversation about the island's wild and windswept cliffs and sheltered inlets she'd photographed the previous day.

The Lakers had never been a quiet bunch, the next generation chips off the old block. The youngest boy slurped noisily as he sucked the very last succulent white meat from inside a claw. Elle picked hers up and did the same.

The child beamed his approval.

"Not bad for a first try," another agreed.

While Kaylie banged her spoon on the tray of her high chair, Elle said, "It's harder than it looks."

"You've got real promise," yet another declared.

"You're not so bad yourselves."

The boys blushed to the tips of their ears.

May sunshine slanted through the old-fashioned picture window. Just beyond that window, forsythias bloomed bright yellow, competing with the sun. A corner of the ocean was visible between the graceful branches of birch trees and wind-battered firs. Inside, cutlery clanged and conversations danced and skipped from one topic to another. All the cooking had made it warm in there, and Mya knew a moment of utter contentment.

She happened to glance across the table, and found Dean looking at her. His eyes were deep blue, his face made up of interesting planes and hard angles. The clatter and clank of dishes and the rise and fall of conversation receded. The years melted away, and it almost felt like old times, as if she and Dean were simply two people sharing something pleasant and ordinary. She smiled, and she swore he wanted to, but he shrugged instead, a marvelous shifting of his shoulders that spoke volumes.

Someone called for the rolls. And everyone and everything else came back into focus. Mya looked away quickly, catching Gretchen and Sylvia in that millisecond before they could avert their gazes.

The meal progressed. When everyone was so full they couldn't possibly eat another bite, dessert was brought out and systematically devoured. Cole was the first to ask to be excused. One by one, the rest of the kids dutifully followed his lead.

Without the children as diversions, nobody seemed to now where to look. Through the sudden awkward silence, Dean's mother said, "You boys better go outside and watch my grandsons. Grady, please try to keep Michael out of the mud. I swear that boy gets more like you every day."

The men stood, carrying a stack of dirty dishes into the kitchen on their way through. When only the women remained, Ruth Laker said, "Pardon me for overstepping my place as guest in your home, Sylvia, but if someone didn't get them out of here, Grady was going to say something profound, such as 'How about those Red Sox?' If you girls would get everything as far as the kitchen, I'll do the dishes."

"You know I'm not going to let you do that, Mother," Sylvia said.

Keeping her face averted, Dean's mother said, "It's good to share a meal with you again, Mya. Would you mind warming Kaylie's bottle for me? I would love to hold her while she drinks it, if that's all right with you, Elle."

Ruth Laker was systematically clearing the room.

Mya's reluctance to leave Elle must have been obvious. In a quiet voice, Gretchen said, "I'll get you a pan. Sylvia's old stove is a little tricky."

In the kitchen, Gretchen took a shallow pan from a low shelf. Adding water, Mya placed the baby bottle in the pan.

"Did you warn Elle?" Gretchen whispered.

Mya shrugged. In truth, Elle hadn't been receptive, saying she preferred to form her own opinions. "Warn her about what? That her grandmother is impossible to love, or impossible not to?"

Sylvia and Gretchen stared at each other. It was obvious the sisters-in-law shared a great deal. It was that way for island women. A photographer whose work was gaining national attention, Gretchen had straight, chin-length brown hair and chic black glasses. Sylvia was a nurse-practitioner. Somebody had teased her about being forty, but she looked years younger, compliments of a pert nose and the freckles across it. The plastic clip at her nape was fighting a losing battle at restraining her curly red tresses. These two women had come from other places to live here. Mya had grown up here, and had left. She wondered what they'd been told about her.

For some reason, she joined the other two, who were staring out the window over the kitchen sink. Reed and Sylvia's backyard was a long sloping expanse of lawn stretching to the enormous gray rocks that made up the shoreline. The grass was green in places, brown in others, thanks to so many dogs, two of which were running in circles around the Laker males. Reed tossed a football and Dean carried four-year-old Dougie on his shoulder the way a lobsterman carried a barrel. Wearing his favorite Red Sox cap, Grady threw a Frisbee to his oldest nephew, the most sullen-looking boy of the bunch.

"How is Cole handling his punishment?" Gretchen asked her sister-in-law.

"As if taking away the car keys has ruined his life and we're prison guards whose sole purpose is to make his existence miserable. How else?"

Mya's gaze went to the oldest boy, almost as tall as the men. He wore a Red Sox cap, too, but his was on backward. She wondered what he'd done.

"Do you know why teenagers are so reckless?" Sylvia asked.

"Because they're stupid?" Gretchen answered.

"I prefer to think of it as a medical condition." Sylvia started the water running in the sink. "Their prefrontal cortex is still immature."

"Their prefrontal what?" Gretchen quipped.

Mya wasn't the only one who smiled.

"Their prefrontal cortex," Sylvia repeated. "It's the part of the brain that controls emotional moderation, organization, planning and judgment. Unfortunately it isn't fully developed at Cole's age."

"So in essence, teenagers are brain damaged."

"That's not the clinical interpretation."

"But it explains a lot, doesn't it?"

Mya thought it would be interesting to know these two.

"The good news is," Sylvia said, "they outgrow it."

"If they live long enough," Gretchen added.

Suddenly, all three were quiet, their ears tuned to what was happening in the dining room. Looking in that direction, Gretchen whispered, "Elle doesn't look sick."

"I know. Surely, that means the chemo is working, right?" Mya thought about how quiet Elle had been these past few days.

"God, Mya," Gretchen said quietly. "I can't imagine what you must be going through."

Mya had assumed they would take Dean's side, blaming her for her decision all those years ago. But as suds filled the sink, they were all mothers.

"Think I should go in there and rescue her?" Mya asked.

"I'd wait until the bottle's warm," Sylvia said.

Gretchen nodded. "She'll be okay until then. Remember, Ruth's bark is worse than her bite."

Kaylie banged the spoon on the wooden high chair. Alone with the woman who was technically her grandmother, Elle didn't know where to look or what to say.

"Bring the baby down here so I can meet you both properly."

Elle wasn't accustomed to being bossed around.

"Don't be bashful," Ruth said, patting the chair adjacent to her.

Lifting Kaylie from the high chair, Elle said, "I've been called a lot of things, but I don't think I've ever been called bashful."

"Are you saying you aren't?"

At Elle's silence, the old woman laughed, the sound loosening the fist that had wrapped around Elle's voice box.

"There hasn't been a child of Laker descent born without a dash of bashfulness and varying degrees of stubbornness. I'm sure you've already discovered those traits in that beautiful baby girl."

Elle took the chair Ruth had specified, settling the baby on her lap. "Kaylie is stubborn, but I think that's a good trait. Last week I couldn't keep hats on her. This week it's shoes."

She was tying Kaylie's shoelaces when she saw the hands reaching so gently toward Kaylie. Her baby stopped wiggling as Ruth trailed her fingertips up Kaylie's chubby arm. From there she felt her way up to Kaylie's hair.

"All three of my babies were bald their first year, and none of them were blond."

For the first time, Elle looked directly into the older woman's eyes. She took a quick, sharp breath.

"They didn't tell you, did they?"

Elle shook her head. And then she shook herself. Ruth Laker was blind.

"I guess Mya was trying to tell me something, but I told her I prefer to form my own opinions."

Ruth nodded. "That's the islander's way, too. We're no strangers to gossip, and if they ever make complaining about the weather a crime, we'll all go to jail. But we leave the truly important discoveries to be made in their own time."

Elle had been trying to imagine what this family had been like twenty years ago, but she couldn't picture it. It was something she'd noticed since her diagnosis. She didn't dwell on the past or imagine the future. At first that had terrified her. But living in fear was no way to live, so instead, she lived in today. And today, Ruth Laker wore a sweater, navy slacks and flat shoes. Her gray hair was short and simply styled, her face not deeply lined. Her brown eyes had probably been beautiful once.

"Something on your mind, child?"

There was a lot on her mind. But Elle said, "How did you know Kaylie's hair is blond?"

Ruth laughed. "How do you think?"

After a time, Elle said, "Dean told you."

"Smart girl. Now, child, what else would you like to hear about?"

In Elle's experience, old people liked to do most of the talking, and yet Ruth drew Elle out of herself. She'd never experienced anything quite like it. They spoke about babies and teething and the ocean and Elle's mother's tragic car accident and Ruth's husband's tragic aneurysm.

"You haven't asked, Elle, but I know you must be wondering about my blindness. My condition has a very long and unfriendly name. Acute zonal occult outer retinopathy. Most people who experience symptoms recover. I didn't. There's always a rainbow, I suppose, and in this instance it's the fact that my blindness isn't hereditary. Here comes Mya with that warm bottle." As if sensing Elle's surprise, she said, "You wouldn't believe the things I hear, feel and smell."

Ruth opened her arms to take the baby. When Kaylie was settled on her lap, she held out her free hand for the bottle. Gently offering it to Kaylie, she said, "It's too nice a day to spend indoors, Elle. I'm sure the others would welcome the chance to get to know you." She turned toward Mya. "If we stall long enough," Ruth said, motioning to the chair Elle had vacated, "Sylvia and Gretchen will have those dishes done."

Dismissed, Elle went outside.

And Mya sat.

It was her turn.

Kids played. Dogs barked. Wind blew and waves broke. Dean knew there was nothing unusual about any of those things, or about the way Reed and Grady ribbed him, or about the way Gretchen and Sylvia watched him, either. It was just another Sunday like a hundred other Sundays on the island.

Liar.

It was May first. Spring was finally in the air. The afternoon was winding down. Soon, it would be time for Mya,

Elle and Kaylie to leave. He hadn't felt dread like this in a long time.

Brad, the resident ocean-watcher, had spotted a pod of dolphins in the cove. Sitting out of the wind with Dean's mom, Elle had continued to rock Kaylie in Reed's favorite Adirondack chair. Everyone else had gone to the lawn's edge for a better look. Discovering an audience, those dolphins had put on quite a performance, jumping and flipping and generally showing off. Eventually they moved on, and Sylvia and Gretchen insisted the boys return to safer ground.

"Are you coming, Mya?" Gretchen asked.

"Hmm?" And then, "Oh. I'll be up in a few minutes."

The others went, but not quietly.

Staying behind, too, Dean watched Mya's gaze return to the ocean. Like Brad, she loved the sea. She'd always said she could never live anyplace else. And yet she'd left. Even as a child, she'd been an enigma. She was afraid of spiders, but not of heights, timid in crowds, but fierce when cornered. He remembered the first time he saw her, and the day they became friends. His brothers had teased him, and his parents had worried. They'd worried about him a lot. It hadn't mattered. He and Mya had been inseparable, "for life," they used to say. They were fourteen that summer when he'd reached for her hand, holding it. That day, their friendship changed. It had taken him six more months to build up enough courage to kiss her.

The hold she'd had on him was strong. Strong enough to last three more years. Strong enough to nearly break him when she left.

He'd hated her for that.

"Whatever you do, Dean, don't make a scene. I'm sure they're all watching."

He hadn't planned to make a scene, damn it. He considered walking away, and leaving her standing there alone, the way she'd left him. He might have been able to do that if he hadn't seen the tears on her face. His mood veered from anger to helplessness.

"Don't mind me," she said. "It's been an emotional day."

She knew. She always knew.

"I saw you talking to Mom," he said. "Did she say something to upset you?"

Mya shook her head. "We had a nice visit." Actually, that conversation *was* part of the reason for Mya's melancholy. It had been beautiful, and she would never forget Ruth's words, or the heartfelt way she'd spoken them.

"I didn't have the chance to say this before you left the island, Mya. And by the time I returned from the Institute for the Blind, you and your mother had gone, your baby had been born, and what was done was done. It was a difficult time for all of us,—Lord, what an understatement—but I never blamed you or held your decision against you."

"Dean blames me," Mya said.

"Does he?"

Mya had done a double take.

And Ruth had said, "Dean has always been fiercely loyal, obstinate and proud, kind and trustworthy, but from the time he was small, there was a shadow in his eyes that terrified me, a deep sadness I could see but couldn't reach. You reached it, but I think even you knew you couldn't fill it."

"He wanted to marry me, Ruth. Keep our baby. I'm not naive enough to believe he's gotten over it."

"Somebody had to do what was best for Elle."

Ruth had made it sound as if she believed Mya had done the right thing. Not even Mya's own mother had ever said that to her.

What was done was done, Ruth had said.

Nineteen years was a long time to hold a grudge, to cast blame. People changed. Mya didn't know Dean anymore, what he thought or how he felt.

She had done what she believed was best. From the moment of Elle's conception, there had been no turning back. Elle's return to Maine had set something in motion, setting a new course for all of them. Once again, there was no turning back.

"Your mom asked me to tell her about Brynn's, and in the process she had me promising to bring her a scarf the next time I visit. And then she asked me what the island looks like today."

She sensed more than saw him come closer. "What did you say?"

They faced the horizon, their arms close but not quite touching. "I told her the sun is glaring off the ocean with so much vehemence it makes your eyes water, then compels you to look again. I told her the dandelions are just starting to pop their heads above the grass and the forsythias are in bloom and the clouds are moving fast from east to west and the new birch bark is pristine white. I told her each of the dogs takes after one of her grandsons, and Grady's oldest looks exactly like you. She chuckled about that."

"I'm glad I'm so amusing."

She felt him looking at her. "How do you know it wasn't a compliment?"

Being on the island again, and describing it to Ruth had brought it all back. Mya had always felt part of the harsh beauty of the rugged shore, the water, the sky and the isolation. It had always seemed that if she stared at it all long enough, it all might make sense. "It's going to be difficult to leave."

"You've done it before."

He blamed her. For leaving. For her decision. For everything. She should have remembered how bad he could make her feel. Forget crying. She seethed. "Of all the -oh, why do I bother? Forget it." She spun around.

He grabbed her hand, halting her.

She almost forgot their audience. Shaking her hand free of his, she stormed to the relative privacy of a small stand of fir trees.

"You make me so mad, Dean Laker. Do you think it was easy for me? Do you think getting over you was easy for me? It took me years. And don't ask me why, either. There's no damn accounting for taste. I'll have you know I didn't stay away all these years to punish you. There. Now are you happy?"

With every I and you she uttered, she poked his chest with one finger. Dean took her hand in self-defense. He'd set out to provoke her. He didn't know why the hell he did that. He'd left her stinking few choices back then. And then he'd blamed her for giving up their child. He'd blamed her because it was easier than blaming himself.

Her hair was tousled, her cheeks pink, her eyes large and brown, and God, her lips. "Happy?" he quipped. "Oh, yeah. I'm rolling in clover. Can't you tell?"

She tugged on her hand. "Well, pardon me all to hell."

He tugged back, gravity and momentum bringing her up against him. It brought a rush of feeling and a stampede of hormones. He heard her take a sharp breath, and then he was lowering his face and covering her mouth with his, all in one motion. With the first brush of his lips against hers, the anger seeped out of him. He kept the contact gentle, drawing the kiss out, and in doing so, it drew some long-buried emotion out of him, as well.

Mya sighed, her lips parting slightly. She knew better than to do this. And yet she couldn't seem to pull away. The kiss was barely a brush of air, a mere hint, like a promise of more, *if* more was what she wanted. God help her, she always wanted more.

Dean kept her off balance. He always had. He could be dark. He could be difficult. By their very nature, they sometimes brought out the worst in each other. And because of that, they'd hurt each other. They'd been bad for each other from the start. She breathed deeply, the pine scent of his aftershave making her sigh. He was bad for her. And yet the shoulder beneath her palm felt solid and strong and good. He was bad for her. And yet the way his chin rasped against hers brought a rush of feeling that resembled joy.

She didn't know who broke the kiss, or if it simply ceased the way it began. "You shouldn't have done that, Dean."

He straightened first, pulling her hands from around his neck. How had her hands ended up around his neck in the first place?

"It will only confuse us," she whispered.

A muscle worked in his cheek. "Old habits are hard to break."

She didn't appreciate being referred to as an old habit, and she bristled. Spinning around, she started back up the way they'd come. He was bad for her, all right. But he brought

out something inside her no other man ever had. She could
have lived out the rest of her days without being reminded
of that.

Elle sat out of the wind, quietly watching the Lakers in-
teract. Ten minutes ago the littlest one had run outside wearing nothing but his T-shirt. Sylvia had chased after him,
scooping him up, laughing as she carried him back inside.
He reminded Elle of her little brother, except Trevor had
Brunhilde, whose pinched expression and open disapproval
in that situation wouldn't have been the least bit funny.
And Dougie Laker had Sylvia. The right mother made all
the difference. She looked at Kaylie, aching.

"Here comes Uncle Dean and Mya." The eldest of the
Laker boys motioned to the pair finally coming up from the
shore. "They must have loved each other an awful lot."

Dean and Mya walked side by side, both stiff, neither
touching. They didn't look particularly cozy. "Why do you
say that?" Elle asked.

"Neither one of them ever married anybody else."

That was the thing Elle had noticed about boys. When it
came to matters of the heart, they were often clueless. And
then, out of the blue, they noticed things that were so obvious women sometimes overlooked them.

Looking around the yard at all the Lakers, Elle wondered
what her life would have been like if she hadn't been

dopted. She tried not to feel guilty for thinking it, and oped her mom understood. Would it have been so bad for Mya and Dean to have kept her? Why hadn't they?

"How long has your grandmother been blind?" she asked.

"She's your grandmother, too," Cole Laker said.

Forget what she'd just thought. Most of the time guys just plain had to be right.

She cast him a withering stare.

He shrugged as if he was accustomed to withering stares. But he said, "I don't know. Since before I was born, I guess. Nineteen or twenty years, maybe."

"Since before I was born, too," she said quietly. She'd watched Ruth Laker a lot this afternoon. The woman moved with such elegance and grace it was impossible to tell she was blind. For some reason, Elle felt a connection, like an age-old kinship with her.

"It must seem weird," Cole said.

She braced herself for difficult questions about her childhood and her illness and her life. "What?" she asked, assuming he would start at the beginning. "Being adopted?"

He made a sound universal to guys. "I should be so lucky. I meant having a kid."

She knew better than to try to explain how much she loved Kaylie to somebody who didn't have any children yet. As if on cue, Kaylie let out a belly laugh. She'd been hauled round by the Laker boys all afternoon, her flowered hat in

stark contrast to so many baseball caps. Elle thought abou
those Red Sox caps Dean had given them. Were she and
Kaylie more Laker than Donahue? More Donahue than
Fletcher?

Kaylie chortled again. Greg had her now. The second
oldest, he had a way with all the other kids. It had taken Elle
a while to tell the boys apart, but Kaylie acted as if she'd
known them all her life.

Her baby was missing a shoe again, her tummy was showing and one pant leg was up around her knee. She'd refused
to take a nap, and would be a grouch tonight. Right now
she was in her glory.

"What is she, like my second cousin?"

Elle thought Kaylie was his first cousin once removed. Or
something like that. "How would I know?" she asked. "Until a few weeks ago, I didn't know you existed."

Surprisingly, he didn't take offense. "We've all heard
about you forever."

Forever.

Elle held her sigh inside. It squeezed through a crack deep
in her chest, crowding in alongside the really bad feeling
she'd been having ever since she'd spoken to her doctor back
home.

Everyone didn't have forever.

CHAPTER 9

Claire tapped the playing cards on Mya's kitchen table and began to deal. "Deuces are wild. Jacks or better to open."

"In English, if you don't mind," Suzette said with uncharacteristic huffiness.

While Claire explained the terminology, Mya settled Kaylie on her lap and opened the new picture book her mother had brought with her tonight.

"Why didn't you just say twos can be anything and you can't start bidding without a pair of jacks?"

"You're the one who wanted to play poker."

With a sigh, Suzette gathered up her cards. "I don't know what's wrong with me tonight. Did I tell you I'm thinking about trying one of those online dating services?"

Claire raised one eyebrow slightly. "Can you spell desperate?"

"There's nothing wrong with a little desperation," Suzette insisted. "Isn't that right, Millicent?"

"Why are you asking me?"

Mya, Claire and Elle all smiled, although Elle's lacked brightness. She looked tired to Mya. Of course she did! The trip to Keepers Island had been draining for both of them. Being back on the island and seeing Dean and all the others had left Mya strangely unsettled.

So, what else was new?

Millie said, "I must admit Sunday nights *have* been a little long since I found out Porter is married. The jerk. I draw the line when it comes to seeing married men, let me tell you."

"Sometimes being a woman isn't easy." Suzette sighed again.

She didn't get any argument there.

"I guess I'm just bored. What would a single man do if he found himself bored and alone on a Sunday night like this?"

Everyone took turns shooting her a certain look.

"You people are disgusting."

"Everything disgusting aside," Millie said, "a man would probably drive on down to his favorite bar, pull up a chair around a table in the back of the room, order a few rounds, smoke a smelly cigar and ante up."

Mya doubted this scenario had much in common with men's poker night. For one thing, the only alcoholic beverages in her refrigerator were wine coolers. And her playing cards had daisies on the backs. And although Millie and Claire chewed on the Cuban cigars Millicent found in her big red purse, they didn't light up because of the danger secondhand smoke posed to Kaylie, who by all rights should have been in bed. They all should have been in bed. Claire and Suzette had school in the morning. Mya had to open Brynn's, Millie her hair salon. For whatever reason, no one was in a hurry to leave.

Lulled to sleep by the drone of the ferryboat's engine and the rocking motion of the waves during the ride from the island, Kaylie had slept the entire way. Wide-awake now, she was making a game of choosing a different lap to sit on.

"Look, Kaylie." Mya pointed at a brightly colored page in the new picture book. "Ball."

Kaylie pointed, too. "Da."

"Are you going to read to your granddaughter?" Millie asked. "Or are you going to ante up?"

Mya did both.

Suzette sighed again. "You don't look old enough to be her grandmother."

"I prefer to think of myself as her nana. Can you say *nana*, Kaylie?"

The baby pointed a dainty finger at another page in the book. "Da."

Everyone laughed as if she'd just discovered the secret of Stonehenge. Elle sat across the table, silently watching. It seemed somebody brought another gift for Kaylie every day. Tonight, she wore the new pajamas Mya had given her. The palest of blues, they had ruffles on the seat and yellow rose-buds on the collar. The colors matched her eyes and hair almost perfectly. Although Mya's eyes were brown, the resemblance *was* uncanny.

Two weeks ago, Mya hadn't known how to hold a baby. Now she did it with ease. "Hit me again, Claire," she said, tossing in two cards before turning her attention back to the picture book and Kaylie.

Elle had been doing a lot of thinking since leaving the island. It was giving her a headache. Her oncologist had said there were still options and plenty of hope. She'd heard that before. While undergoing treatment, she'd met other people who'd heard it before, too. Some had believed it all the way to the end. Reality hung like a thin chill in the back of her mind. She wasn't sure what she was going to do. She only knew she would do what was best for her baby. If she—she couldn't bring herself to think the *d* word. If she *succumbed* to the worst-case scenario, Kaylie would need a family. Elle couldn't seem to get something Cole had said out of her mind. *Neither Dean nor Mya had ever married anyone else.*

Why hadn't they? Could their young love have been the forever kind? Was there such a love?

"Have you seen or heard from Jeffrey?" Suzette asked.

"Jeffrey?" Mya asked. "No. He's probably replaced me by now."

"Like you replaced him?" Elle asked.

Mya shot her a quieting look.

"You've replaced Jeffrey?" Claire asked.

"You're seeing someone else?" Suzette chimed in at the same time.

And Elle said, "Did you leave the stereo on, Mya?"

Suzette wasn't amused or deterred. "Who are you seeing? Don't tell me it's another doctor."

"I'm not seeing anyone."

"She's not lying there," Elle agreed. "She probably had her eyes closed when they were kissing."

Mya gaped at Elle. "You saw us?"

"Then it's true?" Suzette asked.

"Who did Elle see you kiss?" Millie quipped, getting in on the interrogation.

When Mya didn't answer, Millicent repeated the question to Elle. Holding up both hands in a show of innocence, Elle glanced at Mya. "If you wanted it to be a secret, you shouldn't have kissed him in broad daylight where everyone could see."

"I didn't know anyone *could* see us. And I didn't kiss him. He kissed me."

"Who?" Suzette asked.

"Where?" Claire said at the same time.

"On the mouth," Elle said. "Oh, you mean geographically? Where has she been lately?"

Claire and Suzette looked at Elle. They looked at each other. And then they looked at Mya.

"You've been to your island," Claire said drolly.

"It isn't my island."

"You kissed Elle's father, didn't you?"

"He's my *birth* father."

They paid as much attention to the warning in Elle's voice as they had to Mya's moments earlier. Ever droll, Claire said, "This we've got to hear."

Mya moved her cards out of Kaylie's reach. "There isn't anything to tell. Dean and I talked. We argued. Our lips met. And then he basically called me an old habit that's hard to break."

It didn't seem to Elle as if it was an old habit that was hard to break. It seemed to her it was an old feeling that neither of them had been able to fully bury.

"So when are you visiting the island again?" Suzette asked.

Mya looked at Elle. "It's up to you."

Kaylie grinned at Elle from Mya's lap. They really could have been mother and daughter. Feeling small and somehow already forgotten, Elle said, "I don't know."

"Didn't you like them?" Millicent asked.

"They were okay."

"Just okay?"

"They were great, all right?"

"What, then?"

These people were starting to get on Elle's nerves. "I have some things to do first."

"Like what?" Suzette asked.

"Like keep my appointment at Portland Memorial."

Every female around the table stared. Even Kaylie.

Elle wanted to kick herself. But it was too late to take it back. She uttered a word she'd been trying not to say in front of Kaylie.

"You have an appointment?" Millicent finally asked.

Mya said nothing, but her gaze locked with Elle's.

Elle shrugged. She glanced at her cards and tossed in two chips. "I call your bet, Mya. And I raise you ten."

"This appointment," Millicent said, removing her unlit cigar from her mouth. "It's just routine, right?"

She hadn't planned to get into this tonight. "Not exactly."

"What, exactly?" Millie asked a little too loudly.

Elle let her gaze travel all the way around the table. Mya, Millicent, Claire and Suzette stared back at her, waiting, leaving her no way out.

Oh, what the hell. "It seems I'm out of remission again."

Every one of them reacted in her own way, sincerely, completely, with horror and with dread.

"Don't look so stricken," Elle said. "I told you when I arrived I didn't think this round of chemo was working."

"Are you sure?" Millicent asked in a choked voice.

"My doctor ordered some tests before I left Pennsylvania. He called a few days ago with the results."

Mya finally spoke. "You've known for a few days?"

Elle's throat closed up until she could only nod.

Mya tossed down her cards. The others all did the same.

"Are you all folding?" Elle asked.

"Da." Kaylie grinned like the genius she was.

Out of the mouths of babes.

Portland Memorial was spacious and spotless and was filled with stainless steel, state-of-the-art equipment. Intellectually, Mya knew good things happened in hospitals. But the saddest and most difficult thing she'd ever done had taken place in a setting very similar to this one. The whisper of the unknown made today's visit even worse.

Elle sat, terribly quiet and utterly still beside Millicent in a vinyl chair in the reception area in one of the most modern and cutting-edge cancer hospitals in the northeast. Too keyed up to sit, Mya walked the floor with Kaylie. Ever since she'd learned of Elle's illness, Mya hadn't allowed herself to think the worst. She'd done everything she could to keep from thinking about it at all. She'd convinced herself the future had started anew when Elle had knocked on her door a few short weeks ago. It wasn't nearly as easy to be naive here.

They weren't the only people waiting. Wearing a yellow baseball cap to cover her baldness, a woman about Mya's age sat alone on the other side of the room. Not far from her, an elderly man clutched a stainless steel bowl in one hand, his frail wife lending her strength by holding his other hand. Closer were two other women, one middle-aged, one young, both also without their hair. Although ravaged, they were talkative and upbeat. Mya tried not to shy away, but she didn't want to know their stories because then this nightmare would be real.

It was Wednesday, and minutes ticked slowly by. She'd left her part-time clerk in charge at Brynn's. Claire and Suzette promised to relieve her when school let out for the day.

Mya wished Elle would let down her guard enough to allow her closer, but Elle sat in stony silence, invisible barricades firmly in place.

Kaylie discovered some toys in a corner near Elle, and Mya settled down with her to watch her play. Focusing on Kaylie allowed her to think about something besides the horror she was trying to hold firmly at bay.

Dear God. Please.

She knew when Dean arrived, for every head in the place turned. He strode directly to Elle, but said nothing. She could see him making his assessment in one all-encompassing glance around the room.

A name was called. And the woman in the yellow baseball cap rose. Dean took her seat directly opposite Elle. Settling back, he propped an ankle on his opposite knee and jiggled his foot. That lasted for about two seconds before he changed positions, leaned ahead, elbows resting on his thighs, fingers clasped loosely between his spread knees.

Elle finally spoke. "I didn't know you were coming."

His glance at Mya told everyone who'd called him. But like Elle, he said very little.

Kaylie crawled to him. Grasping his pant leg, she pulled herself to her feet then stared solemnly at him without making a sound. Staring back, he was the first to smile. The silent exchange was so poignant Mya bit her lip and had to look away.

A nurse finally called Elle's name. Elle, Mya and Millicent rose. Dean stood last, bringing Kaylie up with him. They all stopped suddenly, uncertain how to proceed.

The friendly nurse said, "The whole family might as well come on back."

Mya waited for Elle to dispute the terminology. Saying nothing, the girl started after the nurse. Scooping up Kaylie's diaper bag, Mya fell into step on one side of Elle, Millicent on the other, Dean and Kaylie close behind. As they made their way through the labyrinth of unfamiliar hallways, footsteps muffled in the carpet, eyes fixed straight ahead so that the subdued and restful artwork lining the walls blurred in their peripheral vision, Mya almost wished Elle had disputed it. This new acquiescence chilled her to the bone.

"This is all I need from you right now, Elle," the perky nurse said after taking Elle's weight, temperature and vitals.

"I'll put the results with your file and tell Dr. Andrews you're here. He's leading edge, and wonderful, but nobody that brilliant has the right to be so handsome, too. We're all madly in love with him. Trust me, you'll drool."

She left them in a spacious room with comfy sofas and snacks and beverages. Helping herself to a soda, Millicent said, "For a second there I thought she was Suzette."

Nobody felt like smiling.

Surprisingly, the doctor didn't keep them waiting long. Shaking hands all around, he patted Kaylie's head last. The nurse was right about one thing. The man was drop-dead gorgeous, but under the circumstances, Kaylie was the only one who drooled.

Bryce Andrews wore his blond hair cropped short. Slightly older than Dean, he'd graduated from Harvard, and he looked it. His shoes were imported, his blue eyes as steady and direct as his approach to his chosen profession. Former college roommates, he and Elle's oncologist back home had kept in touch, personally and professionally, as evidenced by the extent of his knowledge regarding her case. His disappointment that Elle's last round of chemo hadn't been as effective as they'd hoped seemed sincere.

"The lymphoma is knocking on your door again. We're going to try to knock it right back out again. I'm ordering a spinal tap. We'll need to do a bone marrow biopsy but I want to see the spinal fluid first." He spoke of intrathecal medication,

induction, consolidation and new combinations of chemotherapy, and if those failed, stem cell and bone marrow transplantation.

Even Kaylie seemed impressed, sitting quietly on Dean's
lap.

The physician looked at each of them. "We need to move,
but we don't need to panic. Before I continue, do you have
any questions?"

Mya, Dean and Millicent shook their heads, for theirs
wasn't a question they could say out loud.

Elle said, "Are you married, Doctor?"

Other than his Rolex, his only jewelry was a platinum
wedding band that had flashed throughout the consultation. "Yes, I am."

Elle glanced at Mya. "No sense introducing him to Suzette, then."

Elle's attempt at wry humor might have fooled the others, but it didn't fool the doctor. "If I wasn't married, I
wouldn't wear a wedding ring. I don't lie. Period. If you have
questions, ask. If I know the answer, I'll tell you. If I don't
know, I'll find someone who does. I expect the same level of
honesty in return. Do we have a deal?"

He held her gaze for a long time. And then he held out
his hand.

Mya couldn't breathe as she waited for Elle to place her
hand in the hand of the man who was going to save her life.

Finally doing so, Elle said, "We have a deal. I'd like to speak with you privately, Doctor."

Mya, Dean and Millicent all started to protest. Bryce Andrews quieted them all with one shake of his head.

Dean rose first. Settling Kaylie on his arm, he looked at Mya. She wanted to stay, but the stubborn shifting of his shoulders was too insistent to be argued with. As she left Elle alone with the doctor, Mya felt an overwhelming sense of déjà vu.

She really, really, really hated hospitals.

Mya heard her back door open. Recognizing the click of her mother's footsteps, she said hello without turning.

"Any luck?" Millicent asked.

Dragging her gaze away from the nothingness beyond her kitchen window, Mya shook her head. Kaylie was asleep on Mya's shoulder. The last she knew, Elle was napping, too.

After the private portion of her consultation yesterday, Elle had dropped another bombshell. With little inflection in her voice, she'd told them she'd decided not to undergo further treatment. She'd said it as she might have said she'd decided not to order takeout for supper.

"What do you mean?" Millicent had asked.

But Mya said, "For now, you mean."

That wasn't what Elle had meant at all.

"You have to continue treatment," Millie had said.

Elle had fixed her eyes straight ahead.

"Tell her, Mya."

Mya and her mother had wound up arguing with each other.

Finally, Dean had said, "You'll die without treatment."

"Yes, I know." Evidently, Elle had asked Dr. Andrews for the statistics, percentages, time frames. And in that same quiet voice, she'd said, "Chances are, I'll die either way. What difference does it make if I die from the cancer or if I die from the cure? What good is extending my life if I'm too sick to live it? It comes down to quality or quantity."

No amount of arguing, cajoling or begging had budged her decision. Mya had barely slept last night. And when she did, she'd had nightmares. This morning she'd called Elle's adoptive father. After explaining the situation to him, she'd handed the phone to Elle. Even the man who'd raised her, a man who'd won countless arguments in court hadn't been successful in convincing her that she couldn't give up. He wanted her on the next plane home. Elle wasn't going to do that, either.

"What are you going to do?" Millicent asked Mya today.

Mya had thought of little else. Taking a deep breath, she said, "I'm going to talk to her again. And this time I'm not taking no for an answer."

With shaking hands, she handed Kaylie into her mother's waiting arms. Girded with her resolve, Mya marched down the hall and entered Elle's room without knocking.

Elle was just waking up. If Elle didn't appreciate the invasion of her privacy, she made no comment.

In a sudden revelation, Mya understood Elle's tactics. Closing the door partway, she altered hers accordingly and pressed her advantage. "This bullshit you're spouting about this being your life and your choice and your decision? You gave it a good run. Tomorrow, if not today, we're going back to Dr. Andrews and you're going to do whatever he says will give you the best chance of beating this thing. You owe me that much."

Mya could practically see Elle's hackles rising.

"What?" she said. "You think you don't owe me anything? Well I'm sick of that attitude, missy. I gave you life, dammit."

"And then you gave me away."

"Yes, I did. I was in labor for twenty-six excruciating hours. I breathed, I screamed, I begged and I cried. I thought I was going to die from the pain. Walking out of that hospital without you hurt more."

"Grandma Millie says you never mentioned me again."

"That's right. I didn't. I couldn't. What would I have said? I wonder where you are? I wonder what you look like? I wonder if you're happy? I wonder if you ever wished I could have been your mother? I wonder if you hate me? I didn't have to say any of those things out loud. I felt them. Here." She placed a fist to her chest, and then to her stomach.

"Oh, please."

"You don't believe me? You know something, Elle? I don't really care what you believe. You want to hate me, you go for it. Hate me with everything you have. You turn that hatred into energy, and you use that energy to fight. I don't really care what Dr. Andrews told you about your chances, percentages, risks. You know people who've died from the cure? At least they died fighting. You're my daughter, dammit, and my daughter isn't a quitter."

"I'm not your daughter, and you're not my mother."

Tears ran down Mya's cheeks. "So that's what this is about. If you want to punish me for giving you up, find another way. For the record, I gave you up because I believed it was the best thing for you, your best chance for a good, happy life. I always knew I loved you, but I didn't know how much until you came knocking on my front door. You came to me for a reason. And I'm not going to let you die. Do you understand?"

Elle's face was dry, and as white as the curtains at the window behind her. Mya wished she would say something.

"I can't watch you die, Elle."

"If you want Kaylie and me to leave, we will."

If she'd thought playing her trump card would sway Elle, she was wrong. Was there no way to get through to her?

Tears coursed down Mya's cheeks.

She left the room, and nearly walked headlong into Dean.

Mya gasped, but Dean put his arms around her and held her, just held her until she stopped shaking. Over his shoulder, she saw that her living room was wall-to-wall Lakers. Some sat. Some stood. No one said a word. Not even the kids.

Through the roaring silence, a distinguished voice carried with quiet authority. "Mya," Ruth Laker said. "Ask Elle to come out here."

Mya couldn't move. "I don't…she's already…I mean…"

"Don't worry, we won't hurt your baby girl," Gretchen whispered.

"We have something to tell her," Sylvia said.

"And I think she needs to hear it from us," Grady said.

"From all of us," three of the boys said at the same time.

Dean squeezed Mya's hand. Until then, she hadn't realized her hand was still in his. His blue eyes darkened with emotion, his expression one of immovable determination.

Together, they went to get their daughter.

Unlike Mya, who'd barged in a few minutes earlier, Dean knocked.

"Who is it?" Elle said, snide all the way.

Pushing the door open wide, Dean said, "There's someone here to see you."

Her eyes showed surprise. "Tell whoever it is I'm not up to company."

"Get yourself up to it. They came a long way and they're not leaving until they tell you why they're here."

"They?"

Elle looked terribly pale. Despite the tattoo encircling her arm and the one gracing her shoulder, despite the in-your-face stance, and despite the stubborn tilt of her chin, she was far more afraid than she wanted them to believe. In that instant, Mya was overcome with sweetness for this girl.

"Don't worry," she whispered. "It's not the firing squad. It's your family."

Elle floundered. "The Lakers are *here?*"

Mya nodded.

And Elle said, "That's worse than a firing squad."

"If it's any consolation, I agree." Mya knew better than to attempt to smile. "You can either go to them, or they can come in here to you. Dean's right. I get the feeling they won't leave until they've had their say."

"Oh, God."

"Come," Mya whispered. "You can lean on us."

CHAPTER 10

Elle didn't want to face Dean's family today. Her knees were already shaking too much for that. She didn't want to hear what they had to say. She'd made up her mind. It hadn't been easy. But she'd done it. And she didn't need any interfering relatives-by-default coming out of the woodwork, making this even more difficult.

She dreaded looking into each of their faces.

They hadn't left her a suitable choice. She could go out to them, or they would come in here to her. Some choice.

She was nineteen. Did they think she liked what she was facing? Did they think this was the first time she'd faced it? They didn't know her. And they had no right to question her decision or her right to make it.

One look around Mya's living room was all it took for her to know they weren't going to let that stop them. Six of them had squeezed onto Mya's sofa like sardines. Others were perched on the arms of overstuffed chairs, the footstool and the rocker.

Since the moment Elle had met them, they'd never been

able to sit still or be quiet, and yet today every last one of them watched her in waiting silence. Even her cat was looking at her, although he did so from Grady's arms. The traitor.

Ruth Laker had said Elle was bashful. If she could have done so without proving the old woman right, she would have hidden.

Mya stood on one side of her, Dean on the other. She'd explained her reasons to both of them. She'd told them how awful the first round of treatments had been, how sick the chemotherapy had made her. The antinausea drugs hadn't helped, and she'd been too weak to pick up her own crying newborn baby. Losing her hair had been dreadful. Even her eyebrows had fallen out. She'd been so ill she hadn't been able to walk across the room. And it had all been for nothing. Non-Hodgkin's lymphoma was a sniveling weasel of a cancer that was damned difficult to cure. Hell, it was next to impossible. The most a person could hope for was a long remission. She'd already been in and out of remission twice. She'd told Mya and Dean that maybe not everyone was born to grow old. And they'd told the rest of the family, which made them traitors, too.

"What do you want?" she asked, trembling more than she would have liked.

Cole unwedged himself from the others on the sofa. Finding his feet, he struck that cocksure, feet-spread-apart-hips-forward-shoulders-back pose of a guy begging for trouble. "Lakers don't give up."

"I guess that cinches it, then. I'm not a Laker."

Gretchen stood next. Pushing her glasses up her nose, she said, "You're acting like a Laker."

"She's acting like a horse's—ow." Cole rubbed his ribs where they'd been duly poked by his aunt's bony elbow.

Greg, Brad and Mike stood in unison, inching forward as if a large hand was pressed to their backs. The oldest of them went first. "It's going to be hard," Greg said. "The treatment and stuff. Don't think we don't know that."

Brad said, "We'll all help. We'll bring you Popsicles, and sit with you to help you through. And I'll tell you everything I know about the ocean."

Michael went last. "We'll help ya take care of Kaylie, too. She already loves us."

Did they think she didn't know that?

She felt drained, hollow, already lifeless. And this wasn't helping. Millicent entered the room, Kaylie sound asleep on her shoulder. Elle's eyes burned dryly at the sight of her precious baby so angelic in sleep. As if that wasn't bad enough, the smallest Laker cousin took three giant steps toward Elle, counting as he did so.

For crying out loud. Not only was the entire thing scripted, it had been choreographed, too.

And yet there was nothing rehearsed about the way

Dougie tipped his head all the way back in order to look up at her. There was nothing artificial in the way his eyes widened with innocence and emotion. "I'm gonna get my finger poked and maybe other places, too," he said shyly. "Mama says it'll pro'bly hurt, but not real bad and it's okay if I cry but I'm gonna try not to. If my blood matches your blood, you can have some of my mone-barrow."

For once, the older brothers and cousins didn't correct him.

Elle shook with the effort to remain stoic.

Finally, Ruth Laker's voice quavered from the far corner. "That clears it up quite neatly, doesn't it, Elle?"

As far as Elle was concerned, the only thing clear was that this family fought dirty. The kids stepped aside, awarding her a clear view of the matriarch of the clan. It was as if the blind woman knew Elle was looking back at her.

"It doesn't matter who raised you," Ruth said. "It doesn't matter what your last name is. You're family. And we don't let family down. We don't let family choose the easy way out. And we don't let family die if we can help it. I guess you're just going to have to deal with that."

"We love you, Elle," Sylvia said. "Every last one of us."

"We always have," her husband said quietly.

"Without ever knowing you."

"But now that we do know you, we love you even more."

"I guess you're going to have to deal with that, too."

Elle lost track of who said what.

By now they were all standing. Nobody said anything more. Not another word. Not even goodbye.

They left to the sound of shuffling feet and muffled breaths. Dean and Mya went outside with them, and Millie walked into the bedroom with Kaylie. The room was empty. And yet it was as if a part of each of them remained.

Casper wound around Elle's ankles. She scooped him up despite the fact that he was a traitor. Pressing her cheek to his soft fur, she felt it, the welling up, the hot throat and aching chest. She squeezed her eyes shut, holding it in. But it was stronger, squeezing past her tight lids, past her hot throat and aching chest, past all her defenses.

Casper purred. And Elle cried like a baby.

Dean and Mya strode as far as the top porch step.

The boys ambled forlornly toward the vehicles at the curb. Using her white cane, their grandmother followed slowly, her eldest son guiding her. "I'm very proud of all of you," she said.

"Think we got through her thick skull?" Cole asked, his attitude typical for a sixteen-year-old boy still grounded for what his mother called stupidity and his father called worse things.

"Time will tell," Ruth answered.

For four and a half years, Mya had known that Dean's father was gone. She'd attended his funeral on the island, and yet it felt unnatural to see Ruth without Tom. Life went on. It was a fact, but instead of taking comfort in it, Mya shivered. She didn't want her life to go on without Elle.

"Cold?" Dean asked.

She hugged her arms close to her body but said nothing, watching Dean's family prepare to leave. It took two vans to hold them all. When the doors were closed, she said, "You aren't going with them?"

"Not yet."

Mya didn't know what Dean was thinking, but she was pretty sure she knew what he was feeling. She felt it, too. They'd broken each other's hearts when they were kids. There was a place inside each of them that hadn't gotten over it. They'd loved. They'd lost. They'd gone on. And now suddenly they were back where they'd started, older, wiser, but every bit as unsure. They'd been given a second chance to know their daughter. And now life was snatching it away and was trying to take her with it. Mya dreaded this thing they faced.

"Let's go see if we got through to her," Dean said.

"What if we didn't?"

"You get the blanket, I'll get the rope."

It hurt to smile. "You know we can't force her, Dean."

"Yeah, I know."

And that scared them both more than either was prepared to admit out loud.

* * *

Elle was waiting for them inside. Tears had left tracks on her face. But she wasn't crying anymore.

Mya could feel her anger. She literally shook with it, resentment and animosity sparking off her like a shorted electrical circuit.

"I used to fantasize about you two. Can you believe that?"

Mya had hoped. She'd wondered. But no, she hadn't known. Together, she and Dean eased closer.

"You're monsters." Elle said it so loud the cat jumped down. "That's what you are. Every one of you."

"Even Dougie?" Dean asked.

She sniffled. "He was put up to it. But it's only a matter of time. He's a Laker, after all." She held up one hand in a halting gesture. "Don't say it. My name is Eleanor Renee Fletcher. I've never been more glad of anything in my entire life."

"Are you going to let Dougie get poked and cry for nothing?" Dean asked.

Mya gasped. Dean always had known how to go for the jugular.

Elle glared at him. "That's dirty."

"Are you?"

"This sucks." She spun around. When she faced them again, fresh tears wet her cheeks.

"It's liable to get worse before it gets better," Dean said.

"But what Mya said before, about waiting nineteen years to lose you. I can't bear it, Elle."

"I made up my mind, dammit. Damn all of you."

"You know what I think?" Dean asked. "I think you have a lot of fight left in you."

Elle took a shaky breath. Fresh tears began to fall. She didn't know why she was crying. She was just so mad! She thought about the needles and the poison and the hair loss and the vomiting and the chills and the weakness. And the dying.

She thought about Kaylie.

For some reason, she saw her mother's face in her mind. She wondered if her mom had known, in that last millisecond before the crash, that she was going to die. Elle envied her that kind of death. Instantaneous. Complete. Irrevocable. Hers wouldn't be that way. She would linger.

She closed her eyes and tried to imagine oblivion. Instead, she pictured all the Laker kids having their blood drawn. For her. And her eyes wouldn't stay closed. They automatically focused on Dean and Mya. Neither looked as if they'd slept. In fact they both looked like hell. There were bags under their eyes and their expressions were pinched. Elle took no pleasure in that. It occurred to her that she hadn't thought this through as thoroughly as she should have.

She knew more than she wanted to know about non-

Hodgkin's lymphoma. The success rate for extended remissions was far less than for the Hodgkin's variety. For some reason, the immune systems of people with the non-Hodgkin's form stopped recognizing the disease as the enemy, and therefore stopped defending the body against it, allowing the cancer cells to multiply and spread. Except in rare instances, the only cure was a stem cell or bone marrow transplant. Elle had seen those up close. As far as she was concerned, transplantation was more brutal and grotesque than the cancer itself.

"I didn't come here to hurt you, you know," she said.

She could hear Millicent talking to Kaylie in the bedroom. She appreciated all the help, and yet she wondered if she should have left well enough alone and stayed away.

But what about Kaylie? Her baby needed a family.

And what did Elle need?

Dean took a deliberate step toward her. As if realizing she wouldn't be receptive to being touched, he turned and headed for the door.

"You're leaving?" Mya spoke for the first time, and there was panic in her voice.

"I have an appointment to have my blood tested, too." He looked at Elle. "I know you didn't come here to hurt us. But you didn't come here to die, either. Did you." It wasn't a question. He made that abundantly clear.

She covered her eyes with her hands, slowly raking her fingers down her face. "No." She said it so softly they couldn't possibly have heard. Putting more voice into it, she said, "I didn't come here to die. You win."

He and Mya looked at her before they looked at each other. Another time she would have given them credit because they didn't gloat.

"*You're* going to win, Elle," Dean said. "And we're going to help you do it."

At first she thought he was going to leave it at that, but he did an about-face. Crossing the room in four long strides, he wrapped his arms around her and lifted her off the floor, the way a dad would lift his little girl. He didn't swing her around. This wasn't that kind of occasion. He just held her. And Elle held on for dear life.

Sniffling, she buried her face in his neck. He was warm and fit and earthy, and when she breathed, she thought she could smell the ocean. "Mya told me you were a bully."

"I did not!"

Her dignity restored, Elle waited until her feet touched the ground to say, "You should have, because he is."

Dean's grin sneaked up on Elle, closing her throat and bringing fresh tears to her eyes. "Tell everyone thanks."

"Tell them yourself."

Elle glanced at Mya, who shook her head. "You're right. He is a bully. And full of himself. Remind me to tell you what he did to win a fight in the eighth grade."

She wound up giving Mya a tentative smile. And it concerned her.

Elle hadn't planned to feel so strongly about these people whose passion had created her. It had been easier when she'd disliked them, blamed them, resented them. "Why can't life ever be easy?" she asked.

"Hell if I know," Dean said.

Mya answered over her shoulder at the doorway. "I don't think it's easy for anybody. From the moment we're conceived, life happens. And we spend the rest of our days trying to figure out why. When it comes right down to it, every one of us holds on." She paused. "For dear life. I'll be right back."

Dean was already down the steps when Mya stepped onto the porch. She closed the door behind her and said, "That was a close one."

He looked back at her, slowly raking his fingers through his hair. "She's our daughter, all right."

Something unspoken passed between their gazes. Too choked with emotion to voice any of the things she was feeling, she said, "One battle down, a thousand to go."

He nodded, and she swore he wanted to scale those steps and haul her into his arms, to somehow rejoice in this small, magnificent achievement. He wound up looking at her long and hard. Dean had trouble with words. He always had. So he talked around them or did without them.

"I'd better be going. Wish me luck."

"Good luck."

"I hope to God I match."

"So do I."

He started toward a car parked in front of the house next door.

"Dean?"

He looked at her over the roof of his car.

"Use the back door next time," she said. "The front door is for company."

His expression took her back.

And then he drove away.

It had been a long, draining, exhausting day.

Mya used to insist she could never work in a hospital, but as Elle went through test after test, discomfort after discomfort, indignity after indignity, Mya noticed that the doctors, nurses and technicians inflicting the pain and discomfort often had tears in their eyes, too. Mya wanted to make them stop. At the same time, she wanted to grasp each of their hands and thank them for the part they were playing in Elle's treatment and cure.

The worst was the bone marrow biopsy. Mya couldn't watch the procedure during which the doctor inserted a long needle into the back of Elle's hip, extracting marrow from deep inside the center of her bone. It was horrible to watch

Elle's face contort in pain. That hurt far more than Elle's crushing grip on her hand. But Elle endured the invasion, the indignity, the discomfort and the pain with a quiet constraint that humbled Mya.

By the end of the afternoon, Elle had been poked, injected, tested and nearly drained of her blood. It made twenty-six hours of body-splitting labor seem like a stroll in the park.

Beyond exhausted, Elle huddled in a chair with her eyes closed. And Mya wondered if she and Dean were doing the right thing by forcing her to go through this. But the alternative was unthinkable.

Helplessness, worry and the smell of the hospital churned in the pit of her stomach. What else must they face?

Thankfully, Dr. Andrews didn't keep them waiting long.

He entered his private office and quietly closed the door. Mya dreaded what he was going to say. He glanced at the checklist of tests that had been run, riffled through Elle's file, then closed it, setting it aside.

"There," he said, looking at Elle.

"Easy for you to say," Elle said, opening her eyes. "What's next?"

"You have a little wait ahead of you while the lab technicians do their jobs. Meanwhile, I'm prescribing vitamins, exercise and weight gain. The next time I see you, I want there to be more of you. Eat. I'd like to see some color on your cheeks, too. More than anything, I want you to have some fun."

"What?" Elle and Mya said together.

He took off his glasses. That nurse that first day was right. Bryce Andrews was gorgeous.

"Fun," he said. "You remember that, don't you? Go shopping or dancing, or better yet, go lie on a white beach somewhere."

"I hear the weather in Maine in famously harsh until July," Elle said.

He smiled. "I hear that, too. As much as everybody complains about it, why do you suppose so many people stay here?"

"Bullheadedness," Elle answered.

"Watch it," Mya said. She couldn't believe it. They were joking.

The dread lessened.

Dr. Andrews was prescribing a reprieve. Later there would be talk of IVs and a port surgically placed, treatment options and plans, drugs, pills, possible side effects and realistic expectations. But today, Bryce Andrews spoke of different possibilities and pleasant expectations.

"Laugh. Play. Raise some hell if you want to. In fact, I recommend it. It's good for the soul. Any questions?"

"Did you ever raise any hell?" Elle asked.

"I should give you my mother's number."

Mya hadn't planned to like the good doctor. She didn't ask how long this reprieve would last. Right now she wanted to pretend it might last forever.

Evidently, Elle felt the same, because she stood. Dr. Andrews shook both their hands.

Out in the hall afterward, Elle said, "That man is hot."

"Apollo reincarnate?" Mya asked, making her way toward the elevator. "Or Brad Pitt's identical twin?"

"Both."

Mya pushed the down button. Waiting for the elevator to arrive, she said, "Do you feel like taking a vacation? We could go to Greece or Rome or to the south of France. Doctor's orders."

"I know where I want to go."

"You do?"

They crowded into the elevator. As the door slid closed and they began their descent, Mya feared Elle was going to say she wanted to return to Pennsylvania. Nothing could have prepared her for her whispered reply.

"I'd like to spend the next few weeks raising some hell on Keepers Island."

"On the island? The kids who live there think it's the most boring place on the planet."

"All the better. We'll sneak up on them. Turnabout is fair play."

Elle stared straight ahead, her nose a few inches from the door. When the elevator reached the bottom floor, she and Mya were the first out.

"You want to go to the island."

"Yes."

"When?" Mya asked.

"This weekend."

"That gives me two days to make arrangements for someone to help out at Brynn's."

"You're coming, too?"

The large hospital exit door opened automatically with a quiet swish. Out in the May sunshine, Mya's answer was a firm nod.

"Grandma Millie says you never go back to the island."

Mya thought about that. The island was where Elle had been conceived and where Dean still lived. For a long time, memories of both were off-limits. "Never is a long time."

"Tell me about it." Elle retreated into her own thoughts.

And Mya made a mental list of everything she had to do to prepare for the weeks ahead. First, they would need a place to stay. Perhaps they could rent one of the summer cottages. It wouldn't be easy to make arrangements without the islanders' notice.

It was ironic that Elle hadn't gotten over the way Dean's family had barged in on her the day before yesterday. Holding grudges ran in this family. On both sides.

Perhaps even more ironic, they were going to the island, where it all began.

CHAPTER 11

Other than a few rustic hunting cabins in wooded areas and the old hotel downtown, the only places for rent on Keepers Island were the McCaffrey Summer Cottages. Six in all, they overlooked McCaffrey's Cove, named seventy-odd years ago by a lobsterman who'd decided there had to be a better way to make a living, and had proceeded to build these stone island houses for tourists. The tourists hadn't come, and Keepers Island had remained a tree-and mist-shrouded recluse in the Atlantic. Mya could still picture the old fisherman scratching his white beard and shaking his head, grumbling because in his lifetime he'd discovered two surefire ways to go broke.

So many old stories. So many old memories.

They'd bombarded Mya as she'd driven past the brick school, the long-deserted lighthouse, and the cliffs overlooking Eagle's Landing, where for years a pair of bald eagles nested every spring. She wondered if the eagles still lived here.

For the most part, the island looked the same. The summer cottages certainly hadn't changed. They were made of stone, had steeply pitched roofs and symmetrical windows and formed a gentle curve between the road and the shore. Mya didn't know who owned them now, but the realty office in town had handled the details when she'd called to make arrangements for their stay.

The cottage had been cleaned and aired before their arrival. The window glass was wavy, the doorknobs and hardware original, as were the painted wood floors throughout the small story-and-a-half structure. The upstairs consisted of two bedrooms with sloped ceilings. On the main floor was the only bathroom, a small eat-in kitchen and a large, square living room. Elle had chosen the sleeping porch facing the ocean for her and Kaylie.

Pausing in the doorway, Mya said, "Are you hungry?"

Kaylie stopped drinking her bottle long enough to grin at Mya from the center of the double bed. Elle didn't look up at all. "Maybe a little." She started to remove several photographs from the bottom of her bag. As if thinking better of it, she slipped them back inside.

"Are those pictures of you?" Mya asked.

"I guess."

"May I see them?"

Elle hesitated.

And Mya was nearly overcome with yearning to know everything about every stage of Elle's life. "I promise not to laugh."

At least Elle finally looked at her.

Entering the room, Mya didn't apologize for staring. Thin as a waif, Elle was beautiful beyond description. Mya couldn't help smoothing a lock of hair nearly as wispy as Kaylie's away from Elle's forehead.

"How did you wear your hair, before—" She caught herself, for Elle had named one condition before coming to the island. She didn't want to talk about her cancer.

"Before it all fell out? You can say it. I call that my BC era."

Before cancer.

"I wore it short until my mom died, but then Brunhilde wanted it long. How did you wear yours?"

It was the first time they'd broached the subject of their pasts since Elle's initial questions after her surprise arrival last month. "I liked to wear mine short, too. Your grandma Millicent claims she decided it would be best to keep my hair short after I took the scissors to it myself when I was three. I kept it that way until I was seventeen."

Elle regarded Mya's short tresses.

"I let it grow after I left the island. It was shoulder-length until the day you knocked on my door."

"No sh—kidding?" She glanced at Kaylie, who was intent upon drinking her bottle. "Why did you get it cut that day?"

It was Mya's turn to shrug. "Some cosmic force?"

It seemed as though a cosmic force had been at the helm ever since.

They'd pulled into the driveway in front of the old cottage about an hour ago. Although Mya hadn't told anybody they were coming, she knew that if her inquiries into this rental hadn't alerted the islanders, the sight of Millicent, Mya, Elle and Kaylie leaving the ferry in a car obviously loaded for an extended stay would have.

Now Millicent was banging pots and pans together in the kitchen, her new purpose in life to fatten Elle up. God help them, they would probably all starve.

Motioning to the photographs, Mya said, "May I?"

Elle's expression stilled and grew even more serious. "Why not?"

The first photo had been taken at a booth at the mall. It was a black-and-white snapshot of Elle and newborn Kaylie. In this photo, Elle's hair was chin-length and thicker than it was now, her face fuller. But her eyes were as old as time itself.

"It was right after the diagnosis. I wanted Kaylie to know what I looked like."

Staring at the image, Mya was filled with such tenderness. As always, it was mixed with a nagging dread. "It's beautiful. *You're* beautiful."

Elle shrugged one shoulder, and Mya wondered if she'd always been shy. The next photograph depicted Elle as a baby. Not even two years old, she was dressed in red velvet and sat on a tall woman's lap, a distinguished-looking man holding her tiny hand. This had been Elle's family, and this woman was the mother Elle missed.

"Was Renee her first name or her middle name?"

"Her first."

There was nothing more Mya could say about a woman she'd never known. Elle acted as if it was enough.

They wound up sitting at the foot of the bed as she brought out four more photographs. The first was a school picture in which she was missing her front teeth. In the next picture, she looked about eight years old. Her short blond hair was mussed. Laughing with her friends, she wore a blue soccer uniform. In the next one, Elle stood behind the same distinguished-looking man, a different woman and a much younger girl and boy. Both girls' hair was long. Elle looked twelve or thirteen, and so lost.

Elle stared at that photo for a long time before putting it away. Only one remained. It was a picture of Elle and a boy, and had also been taken at a booth at the mall.

"Kaylie's father?"

"I almost threw it away, but then I decided she should have one picture of him."

Since it seemed important to Elle, Mya looked closely at the boy. Although his eyes were blue, they weren't the same blue as Kaylie's. He looked like a thousand other teenagers, unshaven, a little cocky and so, so young. His smile looked genuine, his face pressed close to Elle's. "I can see what you saw in him."

Elle studied the photo. "Are you saying you think he's cute?"

"Don't you?"

Again with that shy shrug. "For an asshole."

They both glanced behind them to see if Kaylie had heard. The baby was sound asleep, her bottle still in one chubby hand.

There were so many things Mya wanted to tell Elle, but the words formed too big a lump in her throat. By the time she swallowed it, Elle had drawn away, and the moment was lost.

Elle returned to her unpacking, a pretty strong hint, all things considered. Reminding herself there would be time to talk later, Mya quietly left the room.

She hadn't gone far when a knock sounded on the side door. Millicent and Elle entered the living room from opposite directions.

"Are you expecting company?" Elle asked.

Mya shook her head.

Millie said, "Care to place a bet as to who our first visitor is?"

Mya opened the door to find Dean standing on the stoop, sawdust on his jeans and a carpenter's pencil in his pocket. He assumed his usual stance, work boots planted, hands on his hips.

Behind them, Millicent said, "Shoot. I would have won that bet, too."

"I take it word's out," Mya said.

His smile caught her in the little hollow at the base of her neck. "You were spotted en route, but that was secondary. Evidently there's a leak in security over at the realty office that rented you this place."

Mya had surmised as much.

"I'm here on a mission. I have strict orders to invite all of you to a party."

"Strict orders from who?" Elle asked.

"What kind of party?" Millicent said.

"When?" Mya said at the same time.

Dean looked at Mya last. There was warmth in his eyes and a lazily seductive gleam that reminded her of how he'd looked at sixteen. Twenty years later, his face was made up of interesting planes and hard angles. His teeth were white and just crowded enough to keep him from looking too pretty. His lashes were long and dark—women never had lashes like that—his chin firm, his skin tan.

"My orders came from Sylvia and Gretchen. They've planned a small gathering to celebrate your arrival." He smiled at Elle. "If that isn't cause for celebration, I don't know what is."

"Where?" Millicent asked.

"On the beach in front of the Harbor House. They're having a clambake."

"More seafood," Elle said drolly.

"When in Rome," her grandmother quipped.

Dean said, "I have to get back to work, but I stopped over to welcome you to the island. Tonight's gathering is come as you are. Mom is cooking up enough linguine to feed the entire island."

He smiled and left without saying goodbye.

Closing the door behind him, Millicent said, "Did he say linguine?"

Mya sniffed the air. "Is something burning, Mom?"

"Oh, my God. Lunch."

The street in front of the Harbor House was lined with cars. Hawaiian music greeted them through the double doors, and Grady handed out leis just inside them. "Aloha," he said.

Mya smelled ganias. Since the is were atfcial, it must have been the cdles buing on every ble. There were at least a hudred pple in the room.

In a low voice, Mlie said, "And to think I amost fell for that 'come as you are' nsense."

Syvia crossed the large room the mment she saw them. Cacing le peing all around, she said, "Loing for sothing?"

"The fatted calf."

Sylvia had a marvelous laugh that made her red curls bounce. "Not bad for two days' notice, is it? We were going to have a real luau, but that ocean wind is just too cool tonight, so we had to move all but the clambake inside. I hope you're hungry, Elle, because you're in for a treat." She hunkered down and smiled at Kaylie.

"Sylvia."

Mya recognized Dean's deep voice behind her. From the corner of her eye, she saw him motion with his right hand as he said, "Gretchen is either guiding an airplane in for an emergency landing or she needs you for something."

Laughing again, Sylvia said, "There are grass skirts on the table in the corner. They're giving hula lessons later. You're in for some fun, Elle. Doctor's orders."

As Sylvia hurried away, Elle turned to Mya. "What did she mean, doctor's orders? How did she know that?"

Mya turned to Millicent. "Yes, how did she know that, Mom?"

"Oh, look," Millie said, reaching for Kaylie. "There's Pattie and Sonia. If you don't mind, I'd like to show off this beautiful baby girl."

Kaylie went readily into her arms, and the two of them disappeared into the crowd.

Shaking her head, Mya said, "And she wonders why I keep secrets."

She could feel Dean looking at her. Not that he was the only one. Mya recognized all but a few of the people present tonight. Most smiled if she caught them staring, and yet she felt as if she were wearing a scarlet letter on her chest.

"I have to say one thing for Sylvia and Gretchen," Elle

said over the Hawaiian music. "They know how to throw a little party."

Dean smiled at Elle. "In case I forget later, I'm glad you could make it. That goes for both of you."

Everything inside Mya started to swirl together. That was all it took for all her regrets to melt into her good intentions. Being back on the island was dangerous. It was as if all the years she'd denied herself access to the corner of her heart she'd closed hadn't happened. It scared her. Even her fear was dredged from a place beyond logic or reason, a place where there were only shimmering emotions and yearnings better off buried.

Reed and his three boys motioned them to their table, where several places had been saved. The moment Mya and Elle and Dean took their seats, they were absorbed into the guffaws and easy camaraderie of this family.

Mya talked. She ate. She even laughed. But it was all surface. She'd been back on the island one day. Already, her defenses were a shambles.

By ten o'clock many of the guests had gone home.

The hula lesson had been a hilarious success, as had the contest that followed. A tie had been declared between Elle and Millie.

Mya had seen Dean go outdoors with Grady a while ago. They stood with other men just outside the glass doors. Although he'd kept his distance after dinner, she'd noticed him watching her.

He felt it, too.

Every so often Millie's laughter carried to Mya's ears. Elle seemed to be having a good time on the dance floor with some of the local teenagers. Mya sat with Sylvia and Ruth. Sylvia's youngest was asleep on her lap; Kaylie was asleep on Mya's. The candles burned low, and Mya took a deep breath.

"Something on your mind, Mya?" In the dim light, it was impossible to tell Ruth Laker was blind.

Actually, there was a lot on Mya's mind. Most of it wasn't the sort of thing she could tell Dean's mother. "Whose idea was this party?"

Sylvia glanced at her mother-in-law and then said, "We've been sworn to secrecy." But she looked through the window where Dean stood.

So. It had been Dean's idea. The knowledge changed something inside Mya. A need was building. She'd gone to great lengths to be independent and strong, and had always denied that she was a needy person. But need was a funny thing. It could hide for years, until one day a woman noticed it squeezing into her thoughts, into her life.

Mya said, "It was a good idea to introduce them to Elle all at once. It probably saved her a lot of awkwardness in the coming weeks."

It was Ruth who said, "Who says he did it for Elle?"

Mya was more apt to say something she would regret than crumble into tears, and yet she had to blink moisture from her eyes. Perhaps that was why she didn't see Reed until he'd lifted his youngest from his wife's arms.

"Are you sure you want to keep this tyrant overnight Mom?" he asked.

"I'm sure. And he's not a tyrant. But if he were, he'd have come by it naturally." Ruth stood. Patting Mya's shoulder on the way by, she said, "It's good to have you back on the island, Mya."

Mya watched them make their way through the maze of tables and chairs and people. Reed carried Dougie, who seemed all arms and legs in sleep. Ruth held Sylvia's arm, listening to something her son was saying. Earlier, Mya remembered thinking that not much had changed on the island. Like his brothers, Grady Laker had been a hellion in his day. Now a family man, he'd grown up, and Ruth had grown older.

Nineteen years older.

Mya felt it again, the welling up and the haunting question. What had she missed?

Since Elle had already made arrangements to catch a ride back to the summer cottage with her new friends, and Millicent had always preferred to fend for herself, Mya rose to her feet and prepared to say a few hasty goodbyes.

"I'm going, Elle," she said as she skirted the dance floor.

"You don't mind taking Kaylie with you?" Elle asked.

"You know Kaylie. Once she's asleep, she stays asleep. I'll put her to bed. Will you be late?"

Elle shrugged. "I doubt it. We'll probably finish this dance, smoke a little pot, have a little sex and be home by three at the latest."

Mya wasn't the only one who gaped.

Elle assumed an age-old stance. "I'm kidding." She tucked the blanket around the sleeping baby in Mya's arms and whispered, "None of that should take more than a few hours."

Mya gaped all over again.

"You heard the doctor tell me to raise a little hell."

"I'm sure he didn't mean—" Mya glanced at Troy, Elle's dance partner. "Do you have pot?"

"Why, do you want some?"

Elle laughed. With a beguiling grin, she said, "I'll be home in a little while. God, Mya, I'm not going to do any of those things."

Troy looked a little disappointed.

As Mya went out the back door, she vowed to hug her mother more often.

Her grass skirt rustled slightly in the breeze. Despite the poor lighting, she recognized Dean easily from the back. She couldn't see who he was talking to, but as she made her way closer, Mya overheard the conversation.

"We're all sorry to hear about your daughter's, well, you know. A shame, somebody as young as her. How horrible this must be for you, Dean, especially now, of all times, when you're finally getting the chance to know her."

"I appreciate that, Heather. If you'll excuse—"

"I just don't know how Mya ever gave her up. Or you, either, for that matter. Sure you two were young. But so?"

Mya's feet froze in the sand.

"I doubt there's another girl on this island who would have done that to you. But then, Mya wasn't born here, was she?"

It took Mya until the count of one to change her plans. Holding Kaylie close, she got the hell out of there.

She noticed the headlights in her rearview mirror a few minutes into her drive. They followed her past the ice-cream parlor, past the harbor, past the school, past Eagle's Landing, all the way to the summer cottage.

She threw the lever in park, turned the key, then practically leaped from the car. "Go away, Dean."

He beat her to the backseat, reaching for Kaylie ahead of her. When he straightened, he had the baby in his arms.

The man never had listened.

He ambled toward the cottage and shouldered his way through the door. Inside, he paused. "Let's get her tucked in before you give me hell."

After flicking on a lamp, Mya led the way to the sleeping porch where Elle had set up the baby's portable crib. Dean placed Kaylie on the daybed first. She seemed even more fragile asleep, and so incredibly innocent. It took both of them to change her diaper, remove her shoes and socks and clothes and get her into her sleeper. Somehow most of the vehemence drained out of Mya during the process.

She was fastening the last little snap when Kaylie opened her eyes. She looked at Dean first, and then at Mya. Her eyelashes fluttered in the middle of her disarming, precious smile.

A dozen emotions expanded in Mya's chest, and every one was bittersweet. This was how it might have been if she'd kept Elle. They might have had a hundred nights just like this one, followed by a thousand more as she grew.

A wish was dredged from a place beyond logic. It came from a place she'd kept locked for a very long time. One look into Dean's eyes, and she knew he'd been thinking about what might have been, too. A muscle worked in his jaw, a precursor to his temper.

But of course, he would be angry!

She spun around.

Like a shadow, he followed her into the living room.

"Don't." She trounced across the narrow room, her grass skirt swishing ridiculously. "Just don't."

Dean wasn't sure what she thought he was going to do.

But he hadn't come here to argue. Why had he come, then? "Just don't what?"

She turned on him. "I missed out, too. Don't think you're the only one. I know you wanted her. Not that I could possibly understand you on a soul-deep level. After all, I was never *really* of the island."

He'd been afraid she'd overheard that.

She was the most exasperating, difficult woman he'd ever met. And yet, watching her eyes, he knew why he'd followed her tonight. She drew him. She always had. Without doing a damn thing, she drew him. Just being in the same room with her sent anticipation and a blinding urgency racing through him.

"That's the trouble with eavesdropping," he said. "You rarely get the whole story. You should have stuck around a few seconds longer and you would have heard the rest of it."

"The rest of it?"

"I asked Heather if her halo ever gets tight. And then I asked her how Tim's crew likes having such a good-looking female oceanography student on board for the summer. It took her mind off you, believe me."

"Do you think Tim and this oceanography student are—"

"I doubt it." Dean hadn't planned to be the one to tell Heather about that intern, but dammit he'd had to do something. "Tim will probably have a lousy night and possibly a lousy summer now that Heather knows, but she'll think twice before talking about you again, at least when I'm around."

Mya stood perfectly still. The lamp behind her threaded her short hair with gold and cast her brown eyes in shadow. He wondered what it was that made her so unique. Whatever it was, all these years apart hadn't changed it. Her eyes could still spark with anger one moment, with laughter the next, and still glowed with something he'd never seen in anyone else. No matter what Heather had insinuated earlier, Mya hadn't always been an outcast. It had taken people a while to accept her at first, but once they had, she'd been well-liked, and one of the most popular girls in school. And then he'd gotten her pregnant. If she'd stayed, they would have blamed Dean. Because she'd gone, she'd become the sinner, he the saint.

Nineteen years ago, he'd been determined to replace her. He'd dated other girls on the island and off. Mya had left him. To hell with her then. But it wasn't that simple. When it came to Mya Donahue, nothing was ever simple.

"You were always putting someone in their place where I was concerned, weren't you, Dean? It must have seemed like a full-time job." The ocean broke far in the distance. Much, much closer, her grass skirt swished slightly as she removed it and tossed it tiredly to a chair. "I guess some things never change."

"In that case I won't apologize for what I'm about to do."

"What are you going to do?"

He wasn't sure who moved closer, but he was very sure of his intentions. "This."

He covered her mouth with his.

CHAPTER 12

He kissed her.

At least that was how it began. One kiss that exploded into desire. It was a possessive meeting of mouths and hunger, an urgent mating of instinct and heat and homecoming. It had been building up to this all evening. Mya had known it, felt it, understood it. But she'd fought it. She wasn't fighting it anymore.

Need filled her, uncurling in places physically unconnected. It had been this way when they were teenagers, too. Theirs was a passion too huge to resist, too intrinsic to question. She'd managed to live without it for nineteen years. She'd even convinced herself she didn't want it or need it. Why would anyone want this tumbling free fall into a crevasse so vast it was bottomless?

Because. There was no other explanation. Just because.

Her head tipped back, her hands gliding around his waist, catching in folds of clothing along the way, seeking, discovering, touching, remembering. And all the while, he kissed her.

* * *

Dean didn't know what the hell he was doing.

Okay, he knew. He was losing himself in Mya. He'd known he was going to kiss her before he'd gotten Kaylie out of that damned car seat. He'd told himself he could handle this, could handle Mya and everything she brought out in him. He'd told himself he was older now, old enough to control his own lust. The problem was, this was more than lust. His throat tightened and his chest constricted. And it didn't matter. Need was all that mattered, and it came from everywhere, from the throaty sounds Mya made when he slid his tongue into her mouth, from the soft skin beneath his hands and from the impression of her delicate bones and muscles. Need came from her lips, soft and wet and full, and from the entire length of her body straining against his.

It wasn't enough.

It would never be enough.

He fumbled with the hem of her shirt and backed up, his elbow crashing into the wall. Some men claimed need made them weak. It made him strong, powerful enough to turn them both in an instant, so that her back was against the wall, his body pressing against hers, seeking, still seeking.

And all the while he kissed her.

And it wasn't enough. It was never enough.

"Oh, Dean. Let me breathe."

He gave her the moment she asked for. But she didn't take

it. Instead, her hands went to either side of his face, and she kissed him. Her lips wet and trembly, her body quavering with need, she kissed him.

He had to have her.

It didn't matter where, on the floor, in her bed or against the damn wall. But he had to have her. And he had to have her now.

He saw her eyes flutter and felt her go slightly still. At first, he didn't understand the reason. But then he noticed it, too. Headlights flickered on the far wall.

Through the roaring din inside his head, he heard an engine idling outside. A car door slammed. Voices called.

"Your mom's back," he said.

Mya heard what Dean said, but she was beyond speaking, beyond reasoning. A moment ago, she'd been all the way past the point of no return. Slowly, the daze was lifting, and somehow the voices outside filtered through. Dean was untangling his legs from hers, and drawing her shirt back up her shoulders. She took over from there, hurriedly buttoning, straightening, pulling herself together.

"God," she muttered. "Some things really don't change."

How many times had Dean's parents or her mother or someone else interrupted them in the nick of time when they were kids? They weren't kids anymore but they were acting like kids.

The back door opened and closed. Only one lamp was on

in here, but it would be enough to illuminate their dishevelment, and enough to embarrass them both.

But Millie didn't come looking for them.

The refrigerator opened and closed. The faucet was turned on and off. And then the kitchen light went out and Millicent's footsteps tapped quietly in the opposite direction and on up the stairs. They both listened for the click of her bedroom door.

Finally, as if attached to the same string, they turned their heads and looked at each other. It would have taken only one small smile, one slight sway, one unspoken invitation from either of them and they would have taken up where they'd left off minutes ago.

Neither extended that invitation.

Not everything had stayed the same after all.

He walked to the door. Holding her ground, Mya took a deep breath.

Before letting himself out, he looked back at her. Whatever had been between them still was. But they weren't kids anymore. Tonight wasn't the night they would make love. Oh, they would. Perhaps tomorrow. Perhaps next week. It was just a matter of time.

If not for the peal of church bells carrying from the hill a mile away, Mya might have slept until noon. Once awakened she was glad, for she didn't want to waste her time sleeping.

She left her hair wet after her shower. Pulling on baggy sweats, her favorite orange T-shirt and thick, yellow socks, she followed the aroma of fresh-brewed coffee.

Millicent was reading the Sunday paper at the table when Mya helped herself to a cup of coffee. Elle was spooning oatmeal into Kaylie's mouth. The baby reminded Mya of a hatchling waiting at the edge of the nest, mouth open wide in anticipation of the next bite.

Millie's newspaper rustled as she turned the page. "Nice party last night," the eldest Donahue said.

Mya made an agreeable sound into her coffee.

Kaylie banged a spoon on her tray, and Millicent said, "Noticed Dean's truck was in the driveway when I got in."

Mya closed her eyes. "He followed me home." Turning around, she found the other three staring at her as if she had egg on her face.

"And?" Millie asked.

"And we argued."

Millicent wet one finger and turned another page. "Things sounded pretty quiet from the kitchen. It isn't usually a good argument that makes a woman look radiant the next morning. Nope, it's usually something else entirely."

Mya was pretty sure Elle was smiling, too. "Are you two having fun?"

They were both still nodding when she heard a noise in the next room. "What was that?"

"By the way," Millicent said, "Dean dropped by."

"He did?"

There was another thunk.

Mya set her cup down hard as realization dawned. "You two are very funny."

They both stopped trying to hide their grins.

Mya couldn't resist touching Kaylie's hair on her way by. "You could have warned me, kiddo."

Kaylie's grin was milky, her favorite word garbled but discernible. "Da."

In the living room, Mya was greeted by the sight of Dean's skinny rear end. The man had great symmetry, she'd give him that, white T-shirt, faded jeans, scuffed loafers and all. Bent at the waist, he was doing something to the back of a big new television in the corner. Boxes and packaging foam were everywhere.

"Having fun?" she asked.

He answered without turning. "Define fun. The DVD player is hooked up, but the surround sound system is giving me some trouble."

"Aren't you supposed to be in church?"

He eased into a more comfortable position down on his haunches. "Unless you count the string of cuss words I just called this cable connector, I haven't done anything to confess."

Everyone was a comedian these days.

"Yet."

The simple clarification fanned the craving he'd started in her last night and drew her farther into the room. Lowering her voice, she said, "When do you think you'll have something to confess?"

His hand slipped off the screwdriver, making a loud and painful-sounding thud. He was cradling his knuckles when he finally faced her. The look that passed between their gazes went back a long time. She'd always held her own with him, always gave as good as she got. And then some. She'd forgotten how invigorating it was.

"What is all this?" She motioned to the electronic equipment.

Eyes as blue as Kaylie's crinkled at the corners as he said, "Elle mentioned she likes to watch old movies."

He was spoiling his little girl. It brought a poignant sweetness and a fear neither dared voice. No matter how many *what ifs* and *what might have beens* were between them, the greatest question was an unspoken one. What if none of them matched Elle's bone marrow?

He cleared his throat. "When I finish hooking this up, I thought you and Elle might enjoy a tour of the island."

A month ago, Mya would have said the idea was absurd. A few weeks ago she would have insisted she wouldn't have enjoyed that at all. A few days ago she would have worried that a walk down memory lane was too dangerous. Leaving him to finish his task this morning, she went to get ready.

Whether by design or happenstance, they had the island to themselves. Dean drove around the perimeter first, pointing out landmarks and telling stories of his misspent youth. Elle wanted to know about every story, every place, every old building, everything. When she asked about the floating markers bobbing on the water's surface, Dean explained. "They're lobster traps. Every fishing family has its own markings denoting who's whose. Lobstermen have been known to draw guns when their traps are tampered with."

"No shit."

Dean laughed. "Lobsters were once so plentiful they washed ashore and people simply picked them up by the bushelful. In the seventeenth and eighteenth centuries they were even fed to the servants."

"Do any of the Lakers lobster?" Elle asked.

He shook his head. "My father was the last, and that was the way he wanted it. It's a hard living, physically and financially. Greg says he's going to resurrect the family business, but I don't know. It can be difficult for rookies to break into. He's determined. Who knows?"

"Do Lakers always get what they want?" she asked.

His gaze met Mya's in the rearview mirror. And she braced herself for his answer.

"We try," he said, then changed the subject.

Elle asked to get out at the school. Since it was Sunday, the building was locked. Artwork hung in many of the windows on the lower level, which housed first grade through eighth. The second story was reserved for those in high school.

Mya remembered the first time she'd set foot inside when she was nine. To this day, she associated the smell of chalk and glue with nerves.

"Are there still eight or ten kids per grade?" she asked.

"Are you kidding?" Elle asked.

But Dean said, "That number has been holding for years."

"There are only eight or ten kids per graduating class?"

Dean said, "There were twelve of us."

Again, his and Mya's gazes met. This time it was Mya who said, "There would have been thirteen, but I left near the end of eleventh grade and finished high school on the mainland."

She could see Elle absorbing everything, and wondered about it. If Dean found it strange, he didn't comment.

"What about college?" Elle asked, sounding like a reporter.

"Nobody falls through the cracks in a school this small," he said. "Although a few of us have tried. Your cousin Cole will be seventeen in August. His SATs were through the roof. Takes after Sylvia in the sciences. If he keeps his act together, the school board will pay to fly him to the mainland to attend advanced classes part of every day next year. He has his eye on Harvard."

"Are the rest of the Lakers smart?" Elle gave the empty swing a push on her way by.

"We do all right."

"What about the Donahues?" Elle asked.

Dean answered. "If Mya would have stayed, she would have been valedictorian of our class."

"I guess Kaylie has a fighting chance in the brain department."

Catching Elle's eye, Mya said, "What about you?"

Her shrug was endearingly shy. "My SATs were through the roof, too."

Mya was filled with a pride she probably didn't deserve. And she sighed.

A large shadow glided across the playground. Elle looked up at the bald eagle riding an invisible current in the sky. Mya looked at Elle. "Are you going back to school when your treatments are finished?"

The question came awfully close to that stipulation Elle had named. But Mya couldn't help it.

"We'll see," was all Elle would say.

Mya's and Dean's gazes met, held, for Elle was even more evasive than usual. A worry she couldn't voice worked over Mya.

Eventually, they got back in Dean's four-by-four. He drove

east along gravel roads, across wooden bridges spanning narrow streams and through lush woods. They saw deer, chipmunks and squirrels. Mya would have liked to know what Elle was thinking as Dean pointed out the remodeling and renovation projects he'd worked on. He didn't stop driving or talking until he reached the top of a long and winding path that led to what the islanders called The Cliffs. There, he got out, and Mya and Elle followed more slowly.

Mya hadn't been up here since she'd left the island. The summer people paid a fortune for the large, Victorian houses near the harbor, but as far as she was concerned, those had never been able to hold a candle to this one.

"We won't get shot for trespassing, will we?" she asked.

"No."

"You're sure?"

"Positive."

Noticing signs of life, Mya asked, "Who lives here?"

"I do."

She was glad he didn't look at her, because she was visibly shaken. Her mother hadn't told her he'd purchased this place. The house was one of the oldest on the island and overlooked the Atlantic. Elle had been conceived on a quilt in a sheltered cove just around the bend below.

Shading her eyes with one hand, Elle said, "Can you see Portland from here on a clear day?"

"Almost." Dean's voice was deep and quiet and had the allure of still waters.

"How can you almost see something?" Elle asked.

He demonstrated. Looking toward the mainland, he said "If you stand still enough, stare long enough, hard enough you can almost see."

Her throat thickening, Mya understood. "Do you do tha often?"

"Not if I can help it."

She understood that, too. Staring toward the island, she'o often had the feeling someone was staring back at her. It hac been as if their gazes had met in the middle, in a way they'o never been able to do.

Mya had called it a cosmic force that had sent her to Rolf's that day she'd gotten her hair cut. But in reality the force behind it all stood between them today. And she was tiring. It filled Mya with dread.

Evidently noticing, too, Dean saved the tour of his house for another day, and took them to lunch at the pizza place on the other side of the island. Over thick crusts smothered in piping-hot pepperoni and mushrooms and melted cheese he and Elle talked. Mya noticed that Elle asked a lot of questions. It felt a little like a job interview. And it bothered Mya

Why, she couldn't say.

Elle was halfway through her third slice when she noticed the guy watching her from across the room. He hadn't been at the luau last night, yet he looked familiar.

She thought back, trying to place him. She'd been in Maine less than a month. Where had she seen him?

He knew her. She would bet her last dollar he was enjoying the fact that he'd recognized her first. She considered asking Dean if he knew the guy. But she had a better idea.

She put down her pizza and pushed out her chair. "I'll be right back."

He watched her approach with an aloofness guys probably thought fooled girls. Elle knew Dean and Mya were watching her, as were several other people in the restaurant, so she kept her voice low as she said, "I know you."

"Do you?" Most guys would have smiled by now.

He pushed a chair out with one foot. She'd had more polite invitations, but she'd had less polite ones, too.

Still deciding, she said, "I'm not sure there's enough room at the table for you, me and your attitude."

He still didn't smile, and it finally dawned on her where she'd seen him. "You're the pizza delivery guy, the one with the bad attitude who brought me a lukewarm pizza in Portland last month."

He shrugged. "A thankless job if there ever was one. Hopefully my student loans and grants will come through for next year and I'll never have to deliver another pizza as long as I live."

She looked a little closer. "I figured you for a high school kid."

"I know what you figured me for."

Damn, he'd surprised her. What was this burgeoning re
gard? Lighting on the edge of the chair, she said, "Are you
from the island?"

"My aunt and uncle live here. Are you?"

She pondered that. "Sort of. So what are you doing here
Visiting your aunt and uncle?"

"I'm shadowing my uncle's lobster route, and later I'm go
ing out on the ocean with a crew of fishermen. He says it'll make
a man out of me. Do you want to hang out this afternoon?"

Now *that* she'd expected.

He was average in height and build. His hair was a little
shaggier than it had been the last time she'd seen him, his
eyes dark, dark brown. He didn't look so nerdy without the
coat and hat bearing the pizza store's logo. That in itself sent
up a red flag. "I can't," she said. "I have to get back."

"Are those your parents?"

She glanced at them. "Sort of."

"Is everything in your life a *sort of?*" he asked.

Something about that observation caught her in the chest
"Here's a definite. I have to get back to my daughter."

She watched his eyes as he took that in, and noticed him
glance at her left hand.

"It's just me and my baby girl."

"And those people who are sort of your parents?"

She'd assumed he would be put off by the fact that she had

a baby. Instead, he seemed a little relieved she was single. And he was still interested. Huh. That was totally unexpected. She needed to put an end to this conversation right here, right now. "I'm only going to be here another week or two."

"I'm only going to be here for the summer," he said. "Sounds like the perfect friendship to me."

He was mocking her. What an attitude.

Rising, she surprised herself when she said, "I'm staying in a summer cottage in McCaffrey's Cove. Do you know where that is?"

"I can find out."

"I'm sure you can." Without saying goodbye or naming a time, she returned to Mya and Dean's table.

"A friend of yours?" Mya asked.

"No. His attitude barely fits in this room." Elle picked up her lukewarm pizza and took a huge bite.

"What's his name?" Dean asked.

She shrugged.

"Want me to find out?"

She gave him one of her looks. "You're kidding, right?" She washed her pizza down with her soda before adding, "He's probably going to stop over this afternoon."

"Why?" Dean asked.

"I *sort of* invited him."

CHAPTER 13

Mya had to force herself to walk up the path leading to Dean's door. Walk, don't run had become her mantra, along with breathe, savor, try not to worry.

Sometimes it was almost effective.

She knocked on the door three times. Breathe. Savor. Try not to worry.

This house had been abandoned when they were kids, the windows boarded up, the porch rotting. She and Dean used to sneak up here, pretending they were running away or were stranded or shipwrecked. Sometimes other children joined them, but most often it was just the two of them.

She'd been thinking a lot about her childhood lately. She'd been thinking a lot about her life.

The sound of waves breaking against the rocky shore drew her around. In the distance the horizon arched, the ocean a deep, dark blue where it met a much paler sky. She hadn't come here to look at the view. She wondered how long Dean had owned this property. That wasn't the reason she'd driven over, either.

Exactly two hours and five minutes after Elle had fallen asleep in the middle of the movie they'd rented on their way back from lunch, Dean opened his door. "Is she still asleep?"

Mya shook her head. "That boy from the pizza place stopped by."

"The nerd?"

"His name's Oliver Cooper, and he's not such a nerd."

"You left her alone with a guy who isn't a nerd?"

Mya refrained from mentioning that Elle was nineteen, had been living on her own for a long time and had a child. "Mom's there."

"No offense, but your mother was easy to dupe."

He had a point. "Kaylie's there, too. You saw how cranky she was. Now she's refusing to take a nap. When she gets like this, there's nothing to do but wait it out. No guy could get ideas when a baby is crying, right?"

He seemed to breathe easier. They stood a foot apart, facing the ocean. If she listened hard enough she could almost hear them as they'd been long ago, two children with nothing to do except while away endless summer days.

"Time stood still, didn't it?" he asked. "What I wouldn't give for it to do that now."

He understood, and it filled her. She wanted endless summer days, wanted time to stand still again. Because of Elle.

Ever since Mya had learned that Elle had cancer, every night fell too soon and every morning broke too early.

In essence, Dr. Andrews had given them all a reprieve. But it would only last a week or two. What then?

Breathe. Savor. Try not to worry.

Mya wanted to talk about her fears, to be reassured that everything would be okay, that Elle would come through this and grow very, very old. But saying it aloud wouldn't make it so, just as Elle's refusal to talk about it hadn't made any of it disappear.

"Would you care for that tour now?"

When she hesitated, he leaned down and kissed her. She didn't close her eyes all the way, and neither did he. The kiss didn't last long enough for that. Last night his kiss had been like the soldering heat that joined metals. Today, the brush of his lips on hers was feather soft and fleeting.

As he drew away, he said, "We'll make the tour a short one."

He understood her sense of urgency, too.

Something was happening, changing between them. They weren't enemies anymore. The cancer was the enemy.

The cancer. And time.

She followed him from room to room on what was perhaps the fastest tour in history. When it was over, she had a vague recollection of heart-pine floors, vaulted ceilings and comfortable though sparse furnishings.

As he reached for his jacket, she said, "Going someplace?"

He nodded a little sheepishly. "To your cottage. Nerds are guys, too. Not even a crying baby can change that. Maybe we can't cure her cancer by sheer will alone, but I can break Oliver Cooper's arm if he so much as touches her."

He was being protective, perhaps overprotective. He looked at her, and although neither of them smiled, they both felt better.

This was why she'd come.

"Peripheral," Elle said.

"Good one," Oliver said. *"Lawyer."*

Elle put both thumbs in the air. *"Realtor."*

He nodded. *"Error."*

She made a sound of disgust in the roof of her mouth. They'd been at it for half an hour and it was getting more difficult to think of words whose very pronunciation was annoying. *"Annoying,"* she said.

"Consanguinity."

She looked sideways at him. "I don't even know what the hell it means but it sounds like you just dropped a tin on a cement floor."

"It means a close relation or connection."

She swore her heart skipped a beat, and it was really starting to tick her off. It was Wednesday. He'd been over every evening this week. Tonight, she was going to tell him to take a hike, figuratively, not the kind they'd just taken to the ocean's edge and back.

"Sounds like Kaylie's still crying," he said as they neared the house.

Tell him, she said to herself. *Get rid of him. Just do it. He's not that great.*

So what if he was the smartest guy she'd ever met? And that attitude. It was almost as bad as hers. That didn't mean she liked him.

"*Irk*," he said.

"Good one. *Humid*." For crying out loud, what was wrong with her?

She knew what was wrong with her. And it began with a big fat capital C. A disease like hers should have been called something offensive that made a person gag just saying it. Scientists never should have called it *Cancer*, the name of a beautiful constellation, and an astrological sign indicating sensitivity and intuitiveness. Cancer wasn't intuitive. It was invasive and vile and vulgar.

As much as she and Oliver had talked this week, they hadn't discussed her disease. But he had to know. A guy who dropped words like *consanguinity* would have noticed how thin her hair was, and surmised the reason.

"*Surmise*," she said.

He smiled. And her goddamn throat closed up.

"*Vegetable*."

She came perilously close to giggling, and Elle hadn't giggled in a long, long time.

"Listen," he said.

"What's wrong with listen?"

"No. Listen."

She did as he said, and she heard the ocean and birdsong and leaves rustling overhead. She *didn't* hear Kaylie crying.

This week Kaylie had decided she was going to walk. She wasn't ready to walk, and every time she fell, she got mad and cried. She'd been fussy all week. Even the cat had grown wary of her and now spent most of his time under Elle's bed where it was safe. Yesterday, Kaylie finally cut a back tooth. Today, she was working on another one. Sometimes rocking her helped. Sometimes nothing did. Tonight, Dean had taken over, and after shooting Oliver a stern and meaningful look, he'd insisted they get some fresh air.

Through the window she could see Dean walking around the room. Kaylie had finally relaxed on his shoulder. He was good with her. Elle had been noticing it all week. All the Lakers were good with her. Mya was, too. But Dean had a way with Kaylie.

Tears stung Elle's eyes.

She reached a hand to the back of her neck just above her hairline and felt the new lump. It reminded her that another day was almost over, and she still had a lot to do. She would be starting treatment again soon. She dreaded it almost as much as she dreaded d—

No. She wouldn't think about that.

She'd promised she would take the treatments. And a promise was a promise.

It all sucked, but that was beside the point.

Rather than risk going inside and unsettling Kaylie, she sat on the top step. It felt good to rest a moment, and she sighed.

Oliver chose a spot a few feet away. "*Effervesce,*" he said.

She shrugged.

"*Durable,*" he said. "*Aluminum. Whirlpool. Disheveled.*"

She couldn't believe she smiled. "You know a lot of annoying words." It figured. "What are you going to college to be?"

"What do you think?"

That was the thing about Oliver. He made her think. "A rocket scientist?"

He made a guy kind of sound. "I'm studying architecture, but I'm going to be a writer."

She looked at him. "Of books?"

He shrugged in that universal guy way. "Maybe. More likely of screenplays."

He had dreams. She tried to remember the last time she'd had dreams, then stopped herself. She had a better idea. Taking a deep breath for courage, she said, "You should write a screenplay about a baby conceived on an island off the coast of Maine."

She could feel him looking at her, but she kept her eyes straight ahead. Pretending a fascination with the ocean, she said, "This baby was born in Brunswick, and was held only once by her young birth mother before being placed for adoption."

A lot of guys would have asked a bunch of stupid questions. Oliver just looked at her. Perhaps that was why she continued.

"Her parents moved their perfect little family to Pennsylvania when she was still a baby. She had an idyllic life until her mother died and her father was so lost he remarried a year later. From then on everything pretty much went to hell for the girl. She became a wild child, experimenting with just about everything. She got pregnant, and when she told her boyfriend, he was beyond shocked. Like he hadn't been there, you know? But he promised to stick by her. And she thought everything would be all right because she had love."

The wind crooned, stirring up a breeze that rustled the collar of her lightweight shirt. Waves broke, crashing against the shore. And Elle said, "They talked about their options and decided on the best one. He held her hand in the waiting room of the abortion clinic. She was shivering, and every sound was magnified, even the echoes. Especially the echoes. And she realized the sounds were coming from inside and the echoes were the emptiness she would always feel if she went through with it."

Elle finally looked at Oliver, but her gaze wandered to the ocean again. "She sat so still on the vinyl chair, and he continued to hold her cold, cold hand. When the nurse finally called her name, she and her boyfriend stood. She was shaking, so he held her, and he told her everything would be okay. It would all be over soon. He said it only once, but it echoed. And echoed. And echoed. And instead of following the nurse, she made a mad run for the door.

"He was right about one thing," Elle said. "It was all over very soon. As soon as she told him she'd changed her mind and was going to have the baby, to be exact. Oh, he stuck around for a couple more weeks, but they argued all the time. He never wanted a kid, he said. And one day he went out. And she knew he wouldn't be coming back.

"And she was so scared. So alone. The hardest part was when she told her dad, and she saw the disappointment in his wise, sad eyes. He tried to help, but he had kids of his own, and an unhappy wife. Every day the girl wondered if she had done the right thing. Then a miracle happened. She felt a flutter. Life! She couldn't freaking stop smiling, and she knew she'd been right in the beginning, when she'd been sure everything was going to be okay because she had love. She loved her baby. And she'd made the right decision. Come what may."

From the corner of her eye, she could see Oliver's Adam's apple moving. He had a long, skinny neck. She'd forgotten he was a nerd.

"That sounds like a controversial movie," he said. "Gripping and moving and thought-provoking. I like it."

Now why the hell did that make her want to grin like an f'ing idiot?

"Then what happens?" he asked.

"She has her baby. The most beautiful and smartest little girl ever born. And she knows it won't be easy, but life is good because she has love."

She met Oliver's gaze. Neither spoke, but she knew enough about guys to know when one was getting ideas. Any second now he was going to kiss her.

Elle leaned closer. Inviting trust and perhaps intimacy, she whispered, "Want to know how the story ends?"

He nodded, his gaze on her mouth.

"She gets cancer and dies."

His eyes widened, and he froze.

She placed her hand on his arm apologetically. "All the great masterpieces have tragic endings, don't they? Take all the creative license with the story you want. Good luck with your screenplays. It was nice meeting you, Oliver. I mean that."

She left him sitting on the step while she slipped soundlessly through the door.

* * *

"You guys don't look like cousins, you know?" Amanda Brown insisted.

Elle and Cole looked at each other and rolled their eyes. Sometimes people said the stupidest things.

It was Friday. Cole's restrictions had been suspended for a few hours while he and Elle took Kaylie for a walk in the stroller Gretchen had dropped off yesterday. Five minutes into the walk, Elle had discovered that Cole was a chick magnet. Or maybe it was just this way on islands. It wasn't as if these teenagers could drive to the next town or to a nightclub in the city. Any activity was better than no activity, and the sight of Cole and Elle pushing a baby stroller along the pier on this warm May evening had drawn a small crowd, and most of them were girls.

Elle was trying to imagine growing up here. More importantly, she was trying to imagine Kaylie growing up here.

"Some of us are watching a movie over at the Ryans' later," Amanda said. "Why don't you two join us?"

Cole's best friend nudged him, but Cole said, "Technically I'm still grounded."

"How about you, Elle?" one of the other girls asked.

They came to the end of the pier and automatically turned around, heading back. "Kaylie's not much for movies."

"Look!" one of the girls whispered. "Here comes that dreamy Oliver Cooper."

Elle *was* looking.

Riding in the front of a battered lobster boat, he looked like the rest of the crew in flannel shirt and baseball cap. Except he carried a video camera, which he aimed at them.

The girls practically went into cardiac arrest over a nerd. High-school girls.

"If that's the kind of guy you find at college, I'm definitely going."

"I heard he's making a documentary."

Cole didn't say anything, but he looked at Elle. There was something about his smile that reminded her of Dean's. Tears stung her eyes and it was starting to tick her off. Everything made her feel like weeping these days, and that made her maddest of all.

Amanda fell into step beside Elle. "I hear that you and Oliver have spent some time together. Are you two, you know, an item?"

Girls like Amanda Brown could make Elle go from sad to annoyed in two seconds flat. If she hadn't been so aware of that lobster boat, she would have thanked the girl for her stupidity because being annoyed was better than feeling sad any day. "No. Be my guest," she said.

"That's what I figured," Amanda said. "What with what you're facing and all, you know?"

If she said "you know" one more time, Elle was going to push her off the pier. Hoping to give the fishermen time to tie up the boat and vacate the pier before she got there, Elle slowed to a crawl.

The others went on ahead. How lucky for Elle, Amanda decided to keep her company.

"I just want you to know," the girl said, as if they were best friends suddenly, "I'm rooting for you. Everyone on the island is. My mom says she doesn't know how your, er, Mya Donahue ever could have given you up. Poor Mr. Laker. Mom says it practically killed him."

Elle could hear the blood rushing through her head. "It wasn't a mutual decision?"

"Why, no. He wanted to marry Mya and raise you on the island. I thought you knew."

Evidently, Elle didn't know shit. "What difference does it make? What's done is done." She felt the lump again, and her fingers shook. She'd assumed Mya and Dean hadn't been in love, or she'd figured they were too young for that kind of responsibility. They sure acted cozy these days. If they'd been anything like that when they were young, they could have kept her. Now that she thought about it, she hadn't ever actually asked why Mya had given her up.

Dean had wanted her. That meant it had been Mya's decision. What was she, too big of an inconvenience?

The more she thought about it, the more ticked she got. To make matters worse, Oliver waited until they were almost upon him to climb onto the pier. Some of the other kids spoke to him as they passed.

The other fishermen left. But Oliver stood between her and escape.

He'd looked at her before without smiling. This was different. He must have known she was waiting for him to leave. He lowered to a piling and made himself comfortable. Not about to let him intimidate her, she held his stupid, piercing gaze.

"Hi, Oliver," Amanda crooned on her way by.

He smiled at *Amanda*. But he spoke to Elle as she passed.

"What did he say?" Amanda whispered before they were even out of hearing range.

"Who cares?" Pushing Kaylie a little faster, Elle didn't repeat it out loud.

But he'd said, "Write that story yourself. Come what may."

Mya was carrying her sandals when she entered the kitchen Saturday morning. She was surprised to find Elle and Kaylie awake, too. "You two are early birds," she said, pouring a cup of coffee.

Elle put Kaylie in the high chair then tried to open the jar of baby food.

"Da."

"I'm hurrying," Elle said. But she couldn't loosen the lid.

"Want some help with that?" Mya opened the jar easily.

Elle mumbled something that might have passed for "thanks."

"Your Grandma Millie and I are catching the first ferry to Portland this morning. I have to do payroll, or I wouldn't go."

"Whatever."

Mya looked more closely at the stubborn set of Elle's chin. "Get up on the wrong side of the bed?"

"What difference does it make to you?"

Mya slipped into her sandals and fastened her watch. Elle had been snippy last night, too. "We're going to miss our ferry if we don't get going. Where's your Grandma Millie?"

"Her name is Millie, not Grandma Millie. And how the hell should I know?"

"Okay, Elle. What's going on?"

"Nothing."

Kaylie ate solemnly, watching them with serious blue eyes.

Keeping her voice soft and her expression gentle, Mya said, "Are you mad at the world, or just at me?"

"Why would I be mad at you? You haven't done anything. Except maybe throw me away. I mean, Dean wanted me, but you probably figured I wasn't worth the trouble."

She finally looked at Mya, and there was such hatred in those dark brown eyes. "Who told you that?"

Elle laughed, but there was no humor in it. "You're not denying it. What difference does it make who told me?"

"It wasn't like that, Elle. Please."

The girl jumped up, spun around, out of Mya's reach. "That's not what Amanda Brown said. Which part isn't true? The fact that giving me up was your idea? Or the fact that Dean wanted to marry you and keep me?"

Elle looked deathly pale. And Mya didn't know what to do. "It wasn't that I didn't want you. It was never that."

"Why don't you tell me what it was then? This I've got to hear."

Millie entered the kitchen just as Mya opened her mouth to speak, only to close it, the words dying on her tongue. Dressed in red and white, Millicent looked from her daughter to her granddaughter. "What's going on?"

Kaylie whimpered. And Elle sat back down. "I didn't mean to get into this. Nothing's going on. You're going to miss the ferry."

"I'll catch the next ferry."

Elle dodged Mya's outstretched hand.

And Mya was bereft.

"It came as a shock, is all," Elle said, without looking at her. "Don't worry about it."

"Elle."

"I mean it. I could use a little space today."

Mya felt her mother looking at her. But Mya's attention was trained on Elle. "I thought you and Kaylie were going to spend the day with Sylvia and Gretchen," Mya said.

"We are."

Meaning she needed a little space from Mya.

A dozen explanations tore through her mind. And she couldn't voice any of them.

"Time's a-wasting," Elle said, snide even now.

"You're sure you'll be okay today?"

"I'm peachy, didn't you know?" Elle looked at Mya and Millie for only a moment. "Just go. Please."

That *please* did it. Although Millicent protested, she and Mya left the summer cottage. Mya's stomach pitched, and tears wet her face.

It wasn't fair.

But then, when had life ever been fair?

CHAPTER 14

It was almost a typical Saturday night on Keepers Island. More than a dozen people, most related to Dean in one way or another, were gathered at Grady and Gretchen's house on Waterwheel Road. Three dogs barked, five boys scuffled and Grady and Reed ignored them the way they always did unless something was broken or someone was bleeding.

Mya and Millie were here tonight, along with Elle and Kaylie. A few weeks ago, Dean wouldn't have believed it was possible, let alone that it could feel so normal. So right.

Michael and Brad had finally enticed Elle to toss a football with them, and were ribbing her because she threw like a girl. Elle took the ribbing without comment, which wasn't like her at all. Something was wrong. Whatever it was had kept Mya quiet all evening, too. Mya didn't get quiet. When she was pushed into a corner, she came out swinging. Either she and Elle had argued, or they needed to. He hadn't decided which it was.

"Dean? Yo. Dean."

He grunted something that meant what.

And Reed said, "You didn't hear a word I said."

"I heard every word you said." He just couldn't remember any of them. His gaze wandered back to Mya and Elle.

"You must be feeling pretty good," Grady said, slapping him on the back. "Elle and Kaylie are both wearing Red Sox caps tonight. Isn't that something?"

It was something, all right.

Earlier, he'd overheard Elle talking to Cole. "A few hundred years ago the Atlantic was so full of lobsters," she'd said, "they used to wash up on shore, and the people simply picked them up by the bushelful." She'd paused. "My father told me that."

Her father. Not her *birth* father. That term always made him feel like a sperm donor. She didn't call him *Dad*. That title was reserved for a dignified though obscure man back in Pennsylvania. She'd said *her father*. The simple distinction had brought a sense of pride and honor, followed by the most humbling sensation.

Across the yard, Gretchen jumped up and hurried into the house, leaving Mya sitting by herself. Dean ambled away from Grady and Reed in the middle of whatever they were talking about.

Mya saw Dean approaching.

He might have been able to fool everyone else with that

slow, lazy gait, but he didn't fool her. His step was deliberate, his gaze very direct.

He lowered his lanky frame into the wicker chair adjacent to hers. Leaning back, knees apart, he asked, "Why so quiet?"

Dean Laker never had been one to beat around the bush. Usually, she appreciated it. Tonight, she didn't know what to say, so she said nothing. She couldn't seem to keep her eyes off Elle. Looking at the girl brought a stirring deep inside, not unlike the flutter kick of her unborn child.

Her child.

Elle's parting words haunted Mya. She'd done what bookkeeping was necessary to keep Brynn's functioning for another week. She'd passed out paychecks and straightened summer sweaters and trendy tanks and dresses. But she was heartsick. Confiding in Suzette and Claire had been a relief, but it hadn't lasted.

"It isn't fair," Suzette had wailed. She'd consulted Mya's personal tides of the moon chart, only to put it away without comment, not a good sign or omen. Mya hadn't needed the stars and moon to know that this was an impossible situation.

"Did you and Elle have an argument?" Dean asked.

"Not exactly."

"What, exactly?"

In the background, dogs barked and boys laughed; waves broke and seagulls fought over something floating in shallow water. The loudest and most aggressive bird won. It was the survival of the fittest. There was no reasoning with instinct, no logic in nature, no gray areas, no looking back or wondering. She envied animals that.

"Mya?"

She finally looked at Dean. His hair was a deep, dark brown, but instead of appearing almost black in the encroaching twilight, the setting sun brought out auburn highlights. There was no reproach in his steady blue eyes, but there was warmth and concern. It reminded her of how he'd looked all those years ago when she told him she was late. She'd been emotional and tearful and so nervous. After about five seconds, he'd said, "It's not the end of the world."

The end of the world had come seven months later.

It felt that way again. Watching Kaylie crawl across the grass toward her, Mya said, "Doesn't she look like a living advertisement for BabyGap?"

Dean spared a glance at the baby, but he was far more intent upon what was going on in the rest of the yard. Elle was quiet. Mya was downright evasive. And across the patio, Millicent was wringing her hands, deep in conversation with his mother.

What the hell had happened between yesterday and today?

* * *

"What are we going to do about our kids, Ruth?" Millicent kept her voice quiet so no one else would hear.

Her heart had been breaking for Mya all day. Her daughter had been quiet during the drive to the ferry dock, and had kept her silence nearly all the way to Portland. She rode on the top deck, her hands gripping the railing, the ocean wind in her expressionless face. Millicent stood beside her, wanting so desperately to help.

"You were right, Mom," Mya had finally said when the mainland came into view. "I should have kept her."

Millie had been waiting all her life to hear Mya say she was right about something. And when it finally happened, Millicent couldn't gloat. She couldn't even agree.

"You did the right thing and you know it!" she'd said.

Mya had taken a shuddering breath. "Did I?"

Millicent had spent the entire day cutting and curling hair for old ladies she'd known since she'd opened her beauty parlor on the mainland. Every one of them asked her what was wrong. Mya didn't believe she could keep a secret, but she hadn't told them. It wasn't until she'd stolen this moment alone with Ruth that she could voice the same question she'd asked nineteen years ago. "What are we going to do about our kids? Dear God, what?"

Ruth Laker sighed. "What can we do, Millie, except love them?"

It wasn't the first time she'd said that, either.

"Parenthood," Millicent said, her heart nearly bursting with love and worry. "It's the best thing and the hardest thing anyone will ever do."

"And just think," Ruth said sagely. "It never ends. Now, tell me what it is that has you, Mya and Elle all tied up in knots."

For a blind woman, Ruth Laker saw an awful lot.

As Millicent opened her mouth, the floodgates opened, too, and everything came tumbling out.

It was dark outside when the knock sounded on Mya's side door. The house was quiet except for an old clock ticking on the kitchen wall. Far in the distance, a foghorn called a lonely warning. Rubbing at the knot between her shoulder blades, Mya took a deep breath, and opened the door.

Dean had donned a jacket since she'd seen him. It was nearly as old and well-worn as the look he gave her as he entered. "You could have told me. You should have told me."

She shook her head. "Let me guess. Our mothers commiserated."

"You should have told Elle the truth."

Again, she shook her head.

"You should have told her I'm the reason you gave her up."

Mya would have staked her life on the belief that this was the first time he'd uttered those words out loud.

"Mya."

Her name was an ache, a whispered plea, a lonesome need filled with past hurt and present acceptance. It knotted Mya's vocal cords and stilled a place deep inside her. "She loves you, Dean. Let's leave it at that."

"The hell I will."

Dean had surprised her. Hell, he'd surprised himself. All those years he'd blamed her because it had been easier than blaming himself. He'd hurt her enough. More than she'd ever deserved. It didn't matter that he'd been hurting just as much, or that he couldn't help it at the time. What mattered was that he didn't hurt her anymore.

"Where's Elle?"

"She's sleeping. Where are you going?"

She followed him into the sleeping porch, switching off the light he flicked on. "What are you doing?" she whispered.

Once his eyes adjusted to the dark, he could see the crib where Kaylie slept, could hear the baby hum in her sleep. By the light of the moon shining through ribbons of fog, he made his way to the daybed beneath the window where Elle lay sleeping.

Placing a hand on her slender shoulder, he shook her gently. "Elle. Wake up."

"Dean," Mya cautioned.

He shook Elle again. These past few weeks, he'd been on the brink of understanding, but it wasn't until tonight that he finally realized just how great a sacrifice Mya had made all those years ago.

"You don't have to do this," she whispered.

"It's either this or take her over my knee."

Elle opened her eyes. "What the hell?"

"Come on." He hauled the girl out of bed.

"What are you doing?" Elle said, cranky.

"You're going to need slippers or shoes, and a coat. I can carry you or you can walk. Either way, you're coming with me."

Elle's eyes were large when she looked at Mya.

And Dean whispered, "Don't worry, honey. I wouldn't hurt you for anything. But there's something I have to show you, and I'm not in the mood for any of your lip."

Next, Dean turned to Mya. "Stay with Kaylie."

"If you were always this bossy, it's no wonder she didn't want to marry you," Elle sputtered.

He shot his daughter a quelling look. She said no more as he took her by the shoulders and steered her toward the living room. Plucking her Red Sox cap from the hook near the door, he didn't say another word, either.

Mya followed them as far as the porch and watched while he deposited Elle in the passenger seat. "Dean? Be careful."

The look she gave him could have been a valiant effort gone bad, or it could have been the rawest expression he'd ever seen. "Don't worry, Mya. I've got her."

* * *

Elle sat stone still in the passenger seat as Dean's Jeep bounced through potholes and spun through sand. Lame music played in the background. He didn't say anything. He probably figured she was ticked.

She had been at first. Who did he think he was, barging into her room and waking her from a deep sleep? But she'd gotten over that almost instantly. What she felt now was different.

They'd been on this road before. She recognized the dips and potholes, and the curves winding up the hill, but it all looked so different with the fog moving in, turning the darkness creamy white. Every so often, eyes glowed in Dean's headlights, some low to the ground, some not. There had always been something about nighttime that she'd liked, something subdued and mysterious and exciting and unknown.

She opened her own door when he stopped in his driveway. He waited for her at the front of the Jeep, falling into step beside her, between her and the incessant ocean wind, as if he wanted to shield her from the cold.

As if he could.

"Okay," she said, unable to contain herself another moment. "What did you want to tell me?"

He opened his door loudly, then held it for her like a gentleman. It occurred to her that he was a study in contrasts. She must have gotten that from him.

Switching on lights as he went, he didn't release her hand until they stood before a tall, antique cupboard in the kitchen. He had to stretch in order to reach the old clasp. The cupboard door creaked as it opened. He pushed things around on the shelf. And then he brought a bottle out of hiding, and placed it on the counter.

It was a bottle of Scotch. Slightly more than half full, it was dusty, as if it hadn't been touched in a very long time.

"You wanted to show me your stash?"

He ran his fingertips over the neck of the bottle reverently, almost like a caress. "I wanted you to look at the reason Mya didn't marry me."

There was a heavy feeling in Elle's stomach. "You drank?" she whispered.

"I haven't had a drink in eleven years, ten months, and four days."

He carried the bottle to his kitchen table. Pulling out a chair for both of them, he placed the bottle between them, and had a seat.

A foghorn sounded sorrowfully somewhere far, far away. And Elle shivered beneath her jacket. Without saying a word, Dean went to the fireplace where he struck a match. Bending at the waist, he touched it to dry kindling.

The fire was just a lick of flames at first, but then it whooshed up, enveloping the logs. Bark crackled, popped. Staring at the flames, he said, "I started drinking when I was fifteen. The guys and I would go down to the wharf, or out to McCaffrey's Cove and pass a bottle. It was all great fun. My brothers tried it. Most kids do."

He returned to the table.

"I told myself I could stop anytime I wanted to. Sometimes I believed my own lies. Back then I was hopelessly angry and too young to know it was normal. I had no reason to drink. My parents didn't beat me or each other. My father hardly drank at all. My girlfriend didn't like it."

He met Elle's gaze in the flickering firelight.

"I had no reason to drink. I had two brothers, a dog, the island and Mya. And a taste for cheap Scotch. I told myself all kids drank. But when the haze cleared, I was the only one who wasn't standing. And then Mya told me she was pregnant with you. And God, I didn't even mind. I felt like such a man, Elle. I mean, I loved her. And she loved me. I promised her I would quit."

His gaze went to the bottle. His mouth watered, even now.

"But you didn't quit?" Elle asked quietly.

"Oh, I quit. Over and over. But never for very long. I broke my promise to Mya time and again. She told me she would give you up for adoption if I didn't get help."

From his jacket pocket, he brought out the Red Sox cap he'd given Elle the first time he'd met her. "I didn't need help. Only losers needed help. Addicts. Alcoholics." Touching the cap's bill, he said, "We were barely seventeen. I wonder what the future looked like to Mya back then."

Elle took the cap with shaking fingers, the only sounds the crackle of the fire, the sigh of the ocean and the beat of her own heart. "Great," she said after a long silence. "Now I'm going to have to apologize to her."

Dean felt such love for this woman-child who was his daughter. "I noticed you'd rather ask for forgiveness than for permission. You're half Laker, all right."

She placed the cap on her head. Adjusting it low over her eyes, she met his gaze. "I'm half Donahue, too."

He nodded, his gaze on the fire, not her.

They sat in the cozy nook, quietly watching the flames, not saying a word. Dean never rushed her. She liked that about him. She had a lot to think about. To sort out. Finally, she said, "Mya's probably waiting for me, huh?"

Dean doused the fire then offered Elle his hand. "She's been waiting nineteen years."

"At least there's no pressure." Nineteen years, Elle thought. She didn't want to make Mya wait until morning.

CHAPTER 15

Mya's shadow glided soundlessly against the living-room wall where headlights flickered momentarily. Outside, two doors slammed, and two sets of footsteps thudded on the side porch.

Elle and Dean both glanced in her direction as they came through the door. Dean didn't look away, the expression in his eyes including her in whatever had transpired between this father and his child.

"I'll leave you two alone." He kissed Elle's cheek, squeezed her hand. And when his gaze next went to Mya, there was a tangible bond between them, stronger than it had been when they were kids, and no less intense.

Elle closed the door behind him. She removed her coat and hung it up. Having run out of diversions, she stood before the rocking chair and slowly removed the baseball cap. Her clothes carried the scent of the ocean breeze and fog and the island. Her hair was mussed, and she still wore the cotton tank and baggy sleeping pants she was so fond of.

"So," she said.

"So," Mya said softly.

"Do Donahues have a traditional symbol of their right of passage, too?"

With a shrug, Mya said, "Nothing as prosaic as the Red Sox."

Elle's smile wobbled as she looked at the baby, her baby, sound asleep in Mya's arms, her bottle nearly empty. "She can hold her own bottle, you know."

"I know. I like to hold her." Tonight, she'd needed someone to hold.

Rising, Mya carried Kaylie back to the sleeping porch where she lowered her gently into a well-worn crib used by all but one of the Laker babies.

"I haven't given her the best life." Elle spoke softly, sadly.

"I disagree."

"Figures."

They stood shoulder to shoulder at the rail, looking at the sleeping child. And Mya thought, this was probably how Elle had looked at this age.

"Dean told me why you did it," Elle said. "I know you wanted me. You didn't stay away from the island to punish him, did you? You did it because you knew you would always yearn for it, and me. I didn't have the strength to give Kaylie up. I thought you were selfish. Turns out it's the other way around."

"All any mother can ever do is what she thinks is best." Doubts. Regrets. And yearning. Ah motherhood. "I've always wondered if I did the right thing. Maybe I shouldn't have given you up."

"Maybe I shouldn't have kept her," Elle said.

"You did the right thing, Elle."

"So did you."

They smiled, and they were filled with such understanding.

Kaylie hummed in her sleep. And Elle yawned. "I think I'll go to bed, too."

And that was that.

Or almost.

"There's something I'd like to do first," Mya whispered.

"What?"

"I'd like to hold my little girl."

There was a moment of awkwardness, but only one. And then Mya's arms went around her daughter's back, and Elle's arms went around her mother's. Mya tried not to hold on too tight, but try as she might, she couldn't keep the tears from running down her face as the feel of Elle soaked into her. Mya was thin; Elle was thinner. Mya was young; Elle was younger. Mya was warm; Elle shivered. Both were five-four, belligerent, proud. Both had made choices that had had far-reaching consequences that continued to impact their lives. Both were too emotion filled to speak.

Elle was the first to draw away. Having no choice but to let her go, Mya thought this must be how it was for all parents. Mothers would always wish they could hold on longer. And children would always grow up too soon.

She'd taken several steps toward the door when Elle said, "You know how everybody says you and I are a lot alike? Maybe that's the Donahue right of passage. Anyway, being like you isn't an insult."

Mya smiled. "That was almost a compliment."

"I'll be more careful in the future."

God, Mya loved this girl. "Good night, Elle."

"'Night." She paused. "Mya."

She couldn't call her *Mom*. She didn't have to. They understood one another perfectly. Mya had had a child, but she'd never been a mother, until now. And now it didn't matter how Elle referred to her: Mom, Mother or Mya. What mattered was that they were family—mother, daughter, alike but different, allies, adversaries and friends, at long last.

Mya picked up the cat on her way into the living room, then nearly dropped him at the sight of Dean on the sofa. Once again, it occurred to her that he looked good on her living-room couch. His jaw was squared, his gaze on her face.

"So," he said.

"So," she agreed.

He rose. Gesturing to the overweight white cat, he said, "I thought you were a dog person."

No one else could have made her smile right then. "So did I." She ran her hand down the length of Casper's back. "A dog would have let me know you were here." Casper purred, utterly content. "Why are you here?"

"Good question."

The wind crooned, a foghorn sounded. And Mya sighed. "Thank you, Dean."

"I didn't do anything I shouldn't have done a long time ago."

He came toward her, all male swagger and masculine intent. He, too, smelled like the ocean breeze and fog and the island. Stopping a hairbreadth away, he bent down and kissed her gently, the cat purring between them.

"I'll see you tomorrow, Mya."

He let himself out while she was still smiling. Headlights flickered on the living-room wall. Tires crunched over the crushed seashell driveway. Mya was falling in love. Or perhaps she'd never fallen out of it. Regardless, she couldn't remember when *tomorrow* had held such promise.

This week, Sunday dinner was at Dean's house. And as he always did when it was his turn to feed this small army, he ordered pizza. As usual, he took a lot of ribbing from his sisters-in-law. As usual, the boys loved it.

It had rained part of the afternoon. Like all true Down East-erners, the Lakers did their fair share of complaining about it, especially the kids, who were confined to the house. It didn't make for a very quiet afternoon for any of them.

Mya didn't mind. In fact, she enjoyed the warmth of the fire, the complaints and the laughter, the rejoinders and the food and the scent of melting cheese, even the pungent odor of damp dogs.

Gretchen had developed the photographs she'd taken all week. Accustomed to being photographed and then being forced to view them, the kids had done so quickly. But Elle lingered over them, utterly silent and serious. Mya wondered what she was thinking.

She knew what Dean was thinking.

Every time his gaze met hers, the pull was stronger. Being in the same room with him sent anticipation and a heady sense of urgency racing through her. If there hadn't been a blind woman, a photographer, four kids, two men and three dogs between them, she would have walked straight into his arms.

She really needed something else to do. She rose at the first whimpers Kaylie made upon awakening from her nap.

"I'll get her." The steely determination in Elle's voice stopped Mya in her tracks.

Everyone else heard it, too, and stopped what they were doing. Even the dogs roused. Mya felt pinpricks of trepidation.

When Elle returned with Kaylie, Dean was at Mya's side.

Kaylie held out her hands to him, and he lifted her easily into arms. Suddenly, Elle didn't seem to know what to do with her hands. Like a warrior without her shield, she moved from one foot to the other. Awkwardly, she cleared her throat.

"Something wrong, Elle?" Ruth asked from a nearby chair.

Elle glanced around the room. Since the eldest Laker had asked, she started with her. "I've spoken to Dr. Andrews."

All eyes were on her. Even the little boys'.

"The test results are in," she said.

"Who matches?" Brad asked.

She shook her head. "Nobody."

"None of our bone marrow matched yours?" Cole stumbled to his feet. "Not even mine?"

His arrogance was overshadowed by the enormity and gravity of what was lurking behind Elle's eyes as she said, "'Fraid not."

"Are they sure?" Millicent asked.

For some reason, Elle's gaze went to Mya. "I'm sure," Elle said.

Elle wasn't prepared for the warmth and weight of Dean's hand on the back of her neck. He squeezed gently, his palm grazing the new lump.

He wasn't prepared, either, for he went perfectly still.

She looked at him. The question in his eyes nearly buckled her knees.

"I was wondering how I was going to tell you."

"Tell us what?" one of the boys asked.

"You know that treatment you all bullied me into agreeing to? It starts again pretty soon."

"How soon?" somebody asked.

"You're leaving?" somebody else said at the same time.

"But you're coming back, right?"

Mya stood on one side of her, Dean on the other. "O course she's coming back," Dean said sternly.

Everybody knew better than to make something of that And Elle said, "I'm taking the early ferry in the morning."

Silence.

Finally, Mya said, "How long have you known?"

"A couple a' days."

"Why didn't you tell us?" Sylvia asked.

Looking around the living room at these people who'd been strangers a month ago, Elle said, "I didn't want to spoil your reprieve."

Evidently, Dr. Andrews wasn't afraid of spoiling anything. He didn't sugarcoat anything, and he sure as hell didn't mince words.

"Okay, Elle," he said. "I believe that covers everything for now. Do you have any questions?"

Elle sat completely still, quiet as a mouse. Mya sat still, too, but she wanted to scream, "Why?" Better yet, "Why Elle?"

Bryce Andrews wasn't one of those physicians who hid behind a heavy desk. He sat in a straight-backed chair opposite a sofa where Dean, Mya, Elle, Kaylie and Millicent were lined up stiffly. The test results were back. As Elle had said yesterday, none of the Lakers matched Elle's bone marrow close enough to be a donor. There were alternatives, the doctor had said, treatments, options. As the hospital scents and sounds closed in on Mya, she concentrated on taking one breath, and then another.

"The lymphoma is getting more aggressive. My treatment plan is aggressive, too. I've reviewed your chart Dr. Patel's office forwarded, and we've conferred at great length. I'm starting you off with intrathecal induction. We'll hit the cancer cells, and hit them hard. We're going to do everything we can to get you back into remission. We'll buy you some time, get you on the allogeneic blood cell transplant list. I have a room reserved for you on the sixth floor. If you have no more questions, you can go to Admitting."

"Today?" Elle's voice quavered.

"This morning."

"I planned to begin tomorrow."

Dr. Andrews shook his head. "Today. By tomorrow, the medicine will already be starting to eradicate those new cancer cells. You can't afford to wait, Elle."

The words held warning, planting doubt and fear where

there was already more doubt and fear than any of them could bear. It was a glorious May morning outside, but a cold dark despair followed Mya as she made her way with Elle, Kaylie, Dean and her mother, down the elevator, through a labyrinth of hallways, to Admitting. Elle's expression was stoic. Mya wasn't fooled. Millicent cried softly. Mya didn't allow herself that luxury. Dean looked shell-shocked. Mya knew the feeling.

Perhaps Kaylie sensed the tension. Or perhaps she didn't like hospitals any better than Mya did. Whatever the reason, she wanted nothing to do with the place, and cried inconsolably. Elle couldn't hold her, and the baby didn't want Millicent or Dean. For once, only Mya would do.

"Take her home," Elle said.

"What?" Mya called over the forlorn cries.

Elle looked up from the papers she was signing, straight into Mya's eyes. "This is no place for a baby." She was choking up, and fighting it so valiantly. "I can't take her home. Would you?"

Mya didn't want to leave her child, not even for this precious baby. She turned to Dean, who was having every bit as much trouble with his voice as Elle was. "I'll stay with Elle, Mya."

Millicent stepped forward. "So will I. We'll all do our part, whatever that is. It'll change from day to day, honey, but we're in this together."

Mya did something she did far too rarely. She hugged her mom.

She left the hospital with Kaylie. Keeping a white-knuckle grip on the steering wheel, she maneuvered through traffic, her foot steady on the gas pedal. Kaylie cried all the way. Alone in the car with the baby, Mya joined in.

The atmosphere in Mya's living room was subdued. She didn't remember a day passing so slowly. Millicent had called several times with updates. And Suzette and Claire came over as soon as school let out for the afternoon. Mya didn't know how she would have gotten through the afternoon and evening without them.

Kaylie had clung to Mya, refusing to warm up to the other women. It was unusual behavior. These were unusual circumstances.

With every tick of the kitchen clock, Mya was reminded of the drip of the chemicals seeping into Elle's veins. Every so often Suzette spouted all the positive words Mya needed to hear. Mya knew things were serious when Claire joined in.

Kaylie had finally calmed down after supper. She'd refused a nap all afternoon, and by eight o'clock, she'd wanted to hold her own bottle, and had only needed to be changed and put to bed.

Mya didn't know what she needed, until a knock sounded

on her door, and Suzette opened it to Dean. He looked as lonely and haggard as she did.

"How is she?" she asked.

"Sleeping. How's Kaylie?" he asked.

"Sleeping."

Since Mya was obviously beyond social niceties, Claire made the introductions while she was steering Suzette toward the door.

Later, Mya would vaguely recall her friends saying goodbye. But right now, she had eyes only for Dean.

For a moment, time stood still.

They started toward each other. Meeting in the middle of the room, they stepped into each other's waiting arms.

CHAPTER 16

Dean had known before he pulled out of the hospital parking lot that he wouldn't be returning to the island tonight. He'd kept his eyes on the street, the horrors of the day buried in his gut, and a single thought in his mind.

Mya.

He hadn't considered the possibility that she wouldn't be alone. Her friends, Claire and, what was the other one's name—Susan or something like that—had taken one look at him and cleared out, so that now it was just him and Mya in a dimly lit room. There was no question, spoken or otherwise, no answer except the one in her eyes as she came to him, her arms going around him, his arms going around her, their lips finding the one thing they both needed.

He'd kissed her often this past week, and every time was an indulgence. This was different. It began full-blown, raw and savage, hard and searching, and so reckless he felt her tremble. Their bodies melded, thighs, bellies, chests, mouths. Desperate for more, they wound up in her bedroom. The place didn't matter. They didn't talk. They barely thought. What they did had nothing to do with discovery, almost nothing to do with giving pleasure or receiving it. Seams tore, buttons popped. That didn't matter, either.

He wanted her. Hell, he'd always wanted her. Tonight wasn't about wanting. It was about having. It was about taking. It must have been the same for her, because she took, too, every bit as demanding as he. Her bare thighs braced against his, her breasts cushioned against his chest, her nipples hard. He was harder.

Mya gasped, responsive and impatient. She was in the center of a whirlwind, a spinning frenzy of giving up control and simply feeling, experiencing, being. There was no time to explore, to arouse, to savor. It was as if Dean understood that doing so would have driven her stark raving mad. The adolescent love she'd known for the boy he'd been, with all its sweetness and sentimentality had turned into something smarter, hotter, riskier. "I'm afraid," she whispered.

"Not of me."

She hadn't considered that. But no, she wasn't afraid of Dean. She was afraid of… She gasped as he made them one, and she didn't finish the thought that had had something to do with Elle.

He was rough. But not too rough. He was a driving force, when a driving force was exactly what she craved. He didn't whisper words of love. And neither did she. Her passion was strong. His was stronger. She fell apart, and still she craved more. More is what he gave her. And more is what she gave him. More open-mouth kisses, more recklessness, more savage abandonment, more passion, more everything. He took it, and gave it all back to her, until she was holding on for dear life. And he was holding on to her.

What they did was too intense to be called making love. They didn't speak of the future. Neither wanted to think about the future. What they did had nothing to do with the future anyway. It had everything to do with this moment. It had everything to do with sex. What they did was their damnedest to tangle the sheets and burn up the shower and the living-room floor and burn off the fear in the pits of their stomachs and in the backs of their minds.

What they did had everything to do with a kind of love at the very core of human nature, the kind of love everyone craved and sought and few experienced. Neither said it out loud. They'd never said, "I do." But they did love each other, and they were committed to each other, and had been since they were kids. Elle's conception nearly twenty years ago had forced them to bypass the rest of their childhoods. Her return had brought them back together in a way they couldn't have done on their own.

Eventually, they stilled. It wasn't that they were sated. They were spent. And together, they finally slept.

In the middle of the night, she woke up to discover the

cat asleep at her feet and Dean's side of the bed empty. She found him standing at Kaylie's crib in a wan shaft of moonlight, watching the baby sleep, as if by guarding her, he could guard Elle.

"God, Mya."

"I know." Taking his hand, she led him back to bed. They came together all over again. This time it was poignant, not savage, slow, not frenzied, a gentle joining of two lost souls finally together again.

Afterward, Dean covered them both. They'd made love when they were still teenagers. Then they'd had to hide, sneak, steal moments for their passion. They'd never spent an entire night together. Until now. Turning her on her side, her back to him, he fit his body close to hers. There was so much he wanted to say to her. He'd always had trouble with words. Touching her tonight had filled in the spaces inside him where words never seemed enough. She'd never asked for words. Once upon a time, she'd wanted *his* word, and that was completely different.

"Mya?" he whispered, ready to give her the one thing, the only thing she'd ever required of him. "I won't let you down this time."

The wind sighed and the house creaked. She must have been asleep.

Out of the darkness, she whispered, "I won't take this lying down."

"I can try, but I have to warn you I'm pretty much spent."
She swatted him.

And he sobered, for he realized she was referring to Elle.
"What are we going to do?"

"We need to go public with our story, with Elle's plight.
Somebody, somewhere *has* to match our daughter's bone
marrow. We'll take it to the press, to the tabloids, to television if necessary. We'll take it to the moon if we have to."

"We'll find the perfect match, Mya. We have to."

And once again, finally, in that darkest hour before dawn,
they both found the oblivion of sleep.

Two days later Dean's and Mya's and Elle's pictures were
on the front page of the "Living" section of the Portland
Daily. Suzette's sister worked at the paper, but she hadn't
needed to pull strings or call in favors. This was exactly the
kind of story the media loved to sensationalize and bring to
its readers.

Wire services picked up the pulse of their story. Within
three more days, the paparazzi arrived on Mya's doorstep
and at Brynn's and on the island. Mya and Dean and Millie
and all the Lakers talked to them. They talked to everybody.
If it meant finding a match for Elle, they would talk to the
devil himself.

Dean and Mya were coming out of the hospital a week
after Elle's treatment began when yet another cluster of re-

porters descended upon them, one of them sticking a microphone in Mya's face.

"How is your daughter?"

"Do you refer to her as your daughter?"

"I understand you gave her up for adoption shortly after her birth."

"Do you regret that decision?"

Mya looked from one reporter to the next, and in a deadpan voice, she said, "I'll tell you what. Go get tested. It only requires a little poke and a tiny bit of blood work. If you match her bone marrow, I'll answer your question. In fact, I'll give you enough for an entire book."

"Is that a bribe?"

Dean took over from there. "It's a promise. Elle needs you. She needs one perfect match. I'm begging you. We're begging you. Please be tested."

The entire clip was aired that very night. Everyone cheered for the stunning woman with the short blond hair and spitfire personality and the dark-haired man with the fierce blue eyes. By the next day, people everywhere were lining up to be tested.

Which was what Mya was telling Elle as she lay in the hospital bed, hooked to a machine that delivered the chemicals into her bloodstream. Mya tried so hard to be positive. It was Aristotle who'd said, "Hope is a waking dream."

Few people could argue with Aristotle. But then, Aristotle

probably hadn't held his child while her slight body was racked with shivers, or while her stomach turned inside out, while she moaned and tried so valiantly to be strong.

Dr. Andrews had said the treatment would be aggressive. In her worst, most violently ill moments Mya was terrified the chemicals would kill Elle if the cancer didn't. The anti-nausea drugs didn't help. Dean, Mya and Millie took turns staying with Elle and Kaylie. They answered the telephone and drove and sometimes they ate and even slept.

Days passed. Elle was so sick she didn't even cry when her hair started falling out. Mya cried. She cried in the middle of the night and on the way to and from the hospital. She cried every time Dean's mother called. But she never cried in front of Elle.

Holding an ice chip to her daughter's dry lips, she wished it was her. Dean was her rock. Nearly two weeks after treatment began, he stood on one side of Elle's hospital bed, Mya on the other. Elle lay on her side, her face resting on her bent arm. She held so utterly still, as if not moving might relieve her horrible nausea.

Witnessing Elle's pain had etched lines beside Dean's mouth. He'd never been good in the face of helplessness. If he cried, Mya's heart would break.

Letting another ice chip melt into Elle's parted lips, Mya said, "You aren't going to believe who called today."

Elle didn't move, but Mya knew she was listening.

"Who?" Dean asked for her.

"The people at *Good Morning America*."

"No shit?"

Mya figured Elle couldn't have said it better herself. "Your Grandma Millie took the call. Evidently, Katie wants us to be guests on the show next Friday."

"What did your mother say?" Dean asked.

In a voice barely loud enough to hear, Elle said, "She probably told Katie's people to call her people."

Mya's gaze flew to Dean's. She'd been wrong. It wasn't him crying that had the power to break her heart. It was Dean, struggling not to that did it.

Three days in a row, a single flower was delivered to Elle's hospital room. Each time, the accompanying card contained only one word. The first day it had been hierarchy. The second was coxswain. Today, it was penurious.

Certain Elle was being stalked, Millicent said, "Who could be doing this? I'm calling the police."

Elle stirred only enough to whisper, "Don't. I know who they're from."

She didn't share the knowledge, but it was the only time Mya had seen Elle smile since treatment began.

Dean, Mya and her mother were taking turns dividing their time between Kaylie and Elle. School was out, and Claire and Suzette had taken over responsibilities at Brynn's.

Grady was handling the Laker Construction renovation project on the island. Everyone was doing everything they could. Mya didn't know how to thank them, and yet she feared everything everyone was doing wouldn't be enough.

She and Dean had gone to New York last week. They'd told their story on live television. Viewer response was overwhelmingly supportive. Cards, flowers, letters and gifts poured in. Sylvia had set up a Web site to handle the overflow.

And yet no match had been found.

Yet, she told herself. No match had been found yet.

Dean went home with Mya every night. Together, they cared for Kaylie and Elle. They spoke with the medical staff. Mya organized bone marrow donor rallies. Elle remained in the hospital. Every day, she grew weaker. And every night Mya and Dean became more terrified. Mya didn't know who was winning, the chemicals or the cancer. And when night was darkest, she stared at the ceiling, dread filling her soul, for she didn't see how Elle would last until a match was found.

The door to Elle's hospital room was closed when Mya and Dean stepped off the elevator. Hoping to cheer Elle, and to restore at least a small portion of her fighting spirit, Mya had brought Kaylie with her today.

They weren't the only ones visiting. Elle's family from

Pennsylvania was here. Call her selfish, but Mya was glad she had the baby to hold, for it gave her something to do with her hands other than scratching Elle's stepmother's eyes out.

Dean and Mya hadn't known the Fletchers were coming. They'd arrived before Mya, Dean or Millie usually got here. Evidently, Elle had seen her father and stepmother both briefly, then had asked to speak to her father alone.

Roberta Fletcher was both petite and pretty, or she would have been if her smile hadn't been as fake as her devotion to her stepdaughter. Evidently the reporter interviewing her liked saccharine, for he seemed to hang on her every word. While her mother blabbered on, the little girl meandered to Kaylie.

"Hi Kaylie," Lauren said. "Remember me? I'm your aunt." Perhaps nine or ten, the child giggled, as if she thought it sounded pretty preposterous.

Setting Kaylie on the floor to play with Lauren, Dean and Mya paced. What was happening in that hospital room? Why had Elle needed to see her other father precisely now?

Whatever was said was private. It must have been very emotional, for Richard Fletcher was wiping his eyes as he left Elle's room. With his graying hair and tweed suit, he looked more like a college English professor than an attorney.

His little boy, Trevor, ran to him. Looking up at his father as if at a mountain, the child said, "Daddy, is Ellie going to die?"

Everyone gasped. Even Brunhilde.

He picked up his son. His gaze going to Mya and Dean, he said, "Not if we can help it."

The two men each sized up the other. And the local news team captured it on film. Shoving a microphone in Richard's face, a reporter said, "We're all rooting for your daughter. How is this affecting the rest of your family?"

While he lowered the boy to the floor, Roberta swooped into the limelight. "We've all been so worried. Her father and I have tried to shield Lauren and Trevor from the horror of what poor Elle is facing. But I know they're as worried as we are about their big sister. Poor thing. Bless her heart, you know?"

Mya could have puked.

Perhaps the reporter was savvier than she'd given him credit for, for without missing a beat, he said, "I understand people everywhere are being tested as potential bone marrow donors. Have you been tested, Mrs. Fletcher?"

Mya bit her lip when Brunhilde, er, Roberta paled. Richard let his wife stammer for another moment before saying, "The children and I have been tested. It was a long shot, we knew, but sadly we don't match, either." He looked directly into the camera. "We have to find a match. Please. I challenge every adoptive parent watching to be tested. For my daughter's sake, I'm begging."

Mya hadn't planned to like him.

Elle's Pennsylvania family, the camera crew and reporter had gone when Dean and Mya tiptoed into Elle's room, Kaylie in tow. Mya intentionally had dressed the baby in the Harley shirt Kaylie had been wearing the first time Mya saw her. It was difficult for Elle to concentrate these days, so Mya wasn't sure the girl would notice.

Kaylie stared at all the machines and the stainless steel, and her young mother in the midst of it all. The baby didn't babble, or smile, or reach for her mama.

Drugs, illness and horrible chemotherapy notwithstanding, Elle noticed. Watching through glassy eyes, she said, "I want you two to take Kaylie."

A long time ago, last month, Mya would have said something flippant, such as "Take her where?"

Dean cradled Elle's hand gently in his. "We'll take her, love her, raise her, baby, if it comes to that. But it won't come to that. Do you hear me, Elle? It won't."

Elle didn't argue. That alone sent a renewed dread all the way through Mya.

"Mya?" Elle whispered.

At first, Mya couldn't answer. Her throat convulsing, she finally managed a hoarse whisper. "I'm here, Elle."

"I want to go to the island."

Mya didn't ask questions. She didn't argue, either. Elle was nearing the end of her first round of aggressive, vicious treatments. Three weeks on chemotherapy, two weeks off. If Elle wanted to spend those two weeks on the island, by God, Mya was going to find a way to give her precious girl what she wanted.

"All right," she whispered. But then her voice grew stronger. "I'll see what I can do."

CHAPTER 17

Dean swung his feet over the side of his bed and carefully rose. Looking back to make sure he hadn't jostled Mya awake, he pulled on his jeans and left his bedroom.

As he had the two previous nights, he stopped at Kaylie's room. From the doorway, he heard the baby noises she made in her sleep.

He paused at Elle's door next. Dr. Andrews hadn't wanted to release her to the island. Even as sick as she was, Elle was a force to be reckoned with. The oncologist had been in contact with Sylvia, who ran the island's medical clinic. After ordering more lab work, he'd finally given Elle the okay to leave. "Under one condition," he'd said, his gaze going to Dean's. "If she develops a fever, a rash or bruises, if the nausea returns or her appetite doesn't, if something doesn't feel right to you, I want her back here within the hour. Understood?"

Dean had nodded. He'd understood all too well.

Elle's nausea had finally subsided when the treatments stopped. The act of transporting her to the island had exhausted her so thoroughly she'd slept twenty hours upon arrival. She looked so fragile without her hair. She continued to be weak, her skin so pale, her eyes too large in her thin, haggard face. Looking at her both broke him in half and filled him with a sense of pride he hadn't known he was capable of feeling.

Dean kept up his vigil. Beneath the cloak of darkness, he waited at her doorway, listening for a sound that—he swallowed—a sound that she was alive. She slept so utterly still, he had to wait minutes for his proof. When it finally came in the quiet whisper of her breathing or the barest rustle of her sheet, or slightest movement of the mattress, he closed his eyes and allowed himself to breathe.

He needed a drink.

He always needed a drink. But last night and the night before, he'd managed to return to his bed where Mya lay sleeping. Tonight, he went silently into the kitchen, opened the tall cabinet, and quietly placed the dusty bottle on the counter.

The clear liquid sloshed invitingly.

Dean tried to wet his lips, but his mouth and throat were dry. Wrapping his hand around the bottle, he lifted it up. He tried to close his eyes, to block out the image, but couldn't. His fingers shook, for he knew he held oblivion in his hand.

Sweat broke out on his brow as he removed the cap. With the sound of his heart roaring in his ears, he felt Mya's arms go around him as the Scotch glug-glugged out of the bottle and seeped down the drain. He didn't know if he'd slain the dragon once and for all, but he'd slain it for tonight.

Bringing Mya around to the front of him, he gathered her close. They stood wrapped in each other's arms, listening to the sounds of night. Taking his cue from the crooning wind, he kept his voice low as he said, "I've been waiting for the right time to do that. There's something else I've been waiting a long time to do."

He released her long enough to walk across the room and remove something from a drawer. Mya missed his arms around her. But he returned to her immediately. Barefoot and shirtless, faded jeans slung low, he looked as haggard as she felt. Worry etched in his handsome face as he stopped directly in front of her, and held out his hand. Turning it palm side up, he slowly opened his fingers.

Both of Mya's hands covered her mouth. Her eyes were on the ring.

He held the ring between his thumb and forefinger. "Will you marry me, Mya? Live with me, laugh with me, argue with me, grow old with me? I promise I won't let you down again."

In the dim light over the stove, the sapphire matched Dean's eyes. Although the stone had been placed in a different setting, she thought she recognized it. "Is that the same sapphire?"

He nodded.

And she all but whimpered, for he'd sold his car to buy it

that long-ago summer. He'd been drunk the night she'd flung the ring at him from across the room.

Tonight, she was too emotion filled to speak. But by God, she wasn't going to cry.

As if he understood that she needed a moment to shore up her emotions and regain her control, he pointed to the new stones on either side of the blue sapphire. "This is Elle's birthstone. And this one is Kaylie's."

Forget holding her emotions in check. Tears ran freely down Mya's cheeks as he slipped that simple ring on her finger. The Star of India wouldn't have held a tenth as much meaning or worth.

"I'll marry you, Dean. Tomorrow if you want."

Their gazes met and held. And with a sense of urgency that drove every waking thought these days, they checked on Kaylie and Elle, then returned to bed where they quietly made love, and then planned their hasty, long-awaited wedding.

"Well?" Mya asked, meeting Elle's gaze in her reflection in the mirror. "How do I look?"

Since Mya hadn't asked Elle how she was feeling—Jesus Marie Christmas, if one more person asked her that, she was going to scream—Elle surveyed Mya.

Actually, she'd seen her looking a hell of a lot better. Her face was drawn, her eyes sunken, dark circles rimming them.

The poor woman was worried sick. And there wasn't a damn thing Elle could do about it. There wasn't anything Elle could do about any of it, except smile weakly and tell Mya the truth. "You make a beautiful bride. How about me? Does my hair look okay?"

Mya stopped fussing with her necklace, with her dress, with her lip gloss and slowly turned. Looking Elle over closely, she said, "Not a hair out of place."

As Elle patted her bald head, Mother and daughter shared a wobbly, watery grin.

A quiet knock sounded on the door. Poking her head inside, Millicent said, "You girls ready?"

They both nodded.

Grinning and sniffling at the same time, Mya's mother settled Kaylie on Elle's lap. The youngest flower girl to be in any wedding on the island, Kaylie grinned beguilingly and pointed. "Da."

Elle carried the single yellow rose delivered that morning bearing a single line. "Mythical, with a lisp." It meant nothing to everyone else, and so much to Elle.

Pushing the wheelchair that held the two girls she loved most in the world, Mya walked regally to the living room where Dean, his family, Claire, Suzette and the new preacher from the church on the hill waited.

Mya would have been satisfied to pay a quick visit to the Justice of the Peace. But she and Dean had so wanted Elle to be present, so they'd brought the local pastor to Dean's house.

Mya Donahue was married in a cream-colored silk sheath Suzette had brought with her from Brynn's. Her maid of honor wore a similar dress in pale pink and a matching scarf to cover her baldness. Dean wore his best and only dark suit, a brother on each side serving as co-best men. The ocean breeze stirred through the curtains, carrying the scent of seawater and dandelions and late-blooming lilacs on this, the first truly warm summer day.

Precious, precocious Kaylie wanted to get down halfway through the short ceremony. Dean didn't even hesitate to take the baby from Elle's weak arms. There she remained, the quietest witness of all, perched on his arm as if it was the most natural thing in the world.

"Do you, Mya Donahue, take this man to be your lawfully wedded husband? Do you promise to honor him, cherish him, love him and respect him for as long as you live?"

Millicent sniffled as Mya said, "I do."

And then the minister turned to Dean. "Do you, Dean Laker, take this woman to be your lawfully wedded wife? Do you promise to honor her, cherish her, love her and protect her for as long as you live?"

Everyone sniffled when Dean said, "I do."

Even Pastor Pete.

Placing a hand on his Holy Bible, the young preacher said,

"With the power vested in me by God and the State of Maine, I pronounce you husband and wife."

Dean kissed his bride with Kaylie in his arms. The Laker cousins elbowed each other. Gretchen snapped pictures. All around Mya, she heard clapping. Bending down to hug Elle, she smiled. Then gasped.

"Congratulations," Elle whispered.

Without conscious thought, Mya placed her hand along the side of Elle's face. Handing Kaylie to his brother, Dean leaned down, too. "What's wrong?"

Elle shrugged.

And Mya said, "She's burning up."

The rest of the congratulations would have to wait. A few months ago a buzz would have resounded through the room. Today, everyone swooped down in silence, helping, hindering, getting in the way. Loving.

Dean and Mya rushed Elle back to the mainland, back to the hospital, back to Dr. Andrews. It seemed it was going to come down to a miracle.

CHAPTER 18

Another week had passed.

Elle was giving up. Mya couldn't even blame her. The entire staff in the oncology wing at Portland Memorial was scrambling, as were Dr. Andrews' colleagues in distant hospitals. It seemed everyone was working to come up with a chemotherapy cocktail that would send Elle's lymphoma back into remission.

They weren't even pretending that the new drugs they searched for might cure her anymore. They were trying to buy her some time, and perhaps send her into remission long enough for a bone-marrow donor match to be found.

Mya hadn't heard much of their story on the news lately. It seemed most people had given up hope.

Including Elle.

Mya and Dean didn't have the heart to bully her. They'd spent the first week of their marriage keeping vigil. With every passing day, Mya left the hospital less often and with greater reluctance.

Dean knew why. And he understood. He shared her fear that every time they left Elle might be the last time. He'd never felt such dread, had never been so completely helpless, not even on that long-ago day when Mya had told him their unborn child deserved better than either of them could give her, not even the day Millicent had called Dean's mother, and Dean's parents had told him the papers had been signed, and the newborn baby he'd never seen had become a part of another family.

He'd gotten blind drunk that day. Getting blind drunk hadn't helped then, and it wouldn't help now.

Nothing short of a miracle could help now.

It was taking its toll on everyone. God, his precious Elle. He was worried about Mya, too. She didn't eat. She rarely slept, and when she did, it was fitful and restless.

Elle was asking for Kaylie.

As he and Mya brought the baby up the elevator, he knew Mya was hoping that seeing Kaylie totter her first steps would give Elle renewed courage to keep fighting. Dean was glad he didn't have to spit. He couldn't have, for he knew Elle had asked for Kaylie to say goodbye.

Up ahead, they could see Dr. Andrews coming out of Elle's room. Dean not only felt Mya's panic, he shared it. They hurried faster, their gazes on the face of every nurse and doctor they passed, watching for an indication that they were too late.

Bryce Andrews nodded as they approached. And Dean and Mya heaved identical sighs of relief.

"Is she better?" Mya asked.

Ever blunt, the doctor said, "No. Her port is in. A colleague and I conferred at great length this morning. There's one more drug I haven't tried. It's a long shot. It's been approved by the FDA, but I haven't used it on another patient."

"Administer it," Dean said.

"I just did."

The men looked at each other. Witnessing the silent exchange, Mya was glad she was a woman. It was a strange thing to be thinking about. Placing Kaylie on the floor near Elle's door, she held out one finger to stabilize the baby, who was still wobbly at walking. Mya was a firm believer in equality between men and women, in equal pay and the fact that one sex's strengths were the other's weakness. As she made her way into her daughter's room, her granddaughter toddling proudly at her side, Mya was glad she was a woman. She was glad she'd been able to carry Elle, to feel her unborn child's first flutter kick, a kick that later nearly put her ribs out.

She was glad to be a woman, glad to have been created, and allowed to carry a child, and bear the pain of giving birth. It was a strength inherent only in women. It took two to create a baby, but as Mya neared the hospital bed, she wondered if it was the pain of pushing, of laboring to bring a child into the world that made Mya strong enough to say, "Look, Elle. Look who's here."

At first Elle seemed too weak to open her eyes. After a struggle, she did open them. Blinking a few times, she must have been trying to focus. It couldn't have been easy, for her fever was dangerously high. These past few days, she'd started talking out of her head.

Today, she knew where she was and who Mya and Dean were. It was the first time she'd seen Kaylie walking.

"Atta girl," she said, too weak to raise her voice above a whisper.

Kaylie teetered, suddenly uncertain. Grasping more tightly to Mya's finger, she righted herself, but didn't take another step.

Mya felt Dean's presence behind her, but all her senses were consumed in this moment, in the silent exchange between Elle and Kaylie, and Kaylie and Elle.

Mya didn't know what Elle was thinking, if the medicine made it possible for her to think at all. Beyond tears herself, Mya said, "Shall we get closer to Mama, Kaylie?"

Kaylie had planted her little sandals.

Swinging the baby into her arms, Mya strode the remaining distance to the bed. "There's Mama," she said, singsongy.

"Ma-ma," Kaylie said, as plain as day.

Mya gasped, amazed and shaken by the baby's first real word. Mama. She'd said it to Mya. Not Elle.

Dean stepped forward. For a moment, Elle appeared dizzy, disoriented. Slowly, she smiled. Her eyelashes fluttered, her eyes seemed to roll back in her head.

"Elle," he said.

"Elle!" Mya begged.

Her eyes focused with apparent difficulty, as if she'd come a great distance. Moving her lips in a weak smile that might have been for any one of them, or all of them, Eleanor Renee Fletcher sighed quietly, and closed her eyes.

CHAPTER 19

Dean unplugged his power saw. Wiping his brow, he stood back to survey his progress on the playhouse he was building in his backyard.

Mya was right. It looked more like a castle.

It was summer again, Dean's favorite season, although Mya claimed he said that about every season on the island. A tanker lumbered toward the horizon, and the midday sun glinted in V patterns on the ocean's surface. Much closer, two dogs chased an aging white cat up the apple tree. On the porch, Mya and her mother were arguing. He smiled to himself, for it was just another day in paradise.

"Look at me, Mommy. Look at me, Grandma!"

Dean's smile grew as his gaze rested on the blond-haired little girl doing a clumsy forward roll before her audience of two. It was hard to believe this precious, precocious child who was so much like her mother would be starting school this fall.

"No doubt about it," Millicent said loudly, lowering into a wicker chair. "That child's going to be a ballerina."

"An Olympic champion, you mean," Mya countered.

"A ballerina."

"The Olympics."

"The ballet."

And so it went.

"Daddy?" Eyes as blue as his own looked up at him. "Do they ever quit?"

Dean chuckled, for he never knew what was going to come out of this child's mouth. But the truth was, he'd asked himself that same question a hundred times.

"It's how they say I love you, short stuff." It must have been genetic. Why else would the Donahue women be so obstinate and argumentative? He happened to know from experience that this child only looked cherubic. At three, she'd been able to outargue her Grandma Millie. And she was getting pretty good at holding her own with Mya. Dean was putty in her hand.

A car door slammed. Voices carried. Tails wagging, the dogs left their watch posts beneath the tree to investigate.

Dean and Mya shared a look from across the yard, turning as their daughter yelled to a child equally as precocious as she was. "Quit telling your Mom you love her and come play with me!"

"Just because you're my aunt doesn't mean you can boss me." But Kaylie strutted over to help Cora coax the cat down from the tree.

Mya sidled up to Dean's right side, their eldest daughter

to his left. Unable to stand the suspense a moment longer, he said, "Well?"

Elle struck a pose. The earrings and nose rings were gone, but her spunk was stronger than ever as she said, "They about drained me of my blood, but I'm good to go for another year."

"Thank God," Millicent said.

"Amen to that," Mya whispered.

Elle wore her hair chin-length now. It had grown back wavy and had darkened to a honey blond. She was smart and quick and still a spitfire. Coming back from the brink of death had left her with a depth that far surpassed most women at the tender age of twenty-five.

The smile she gave to Dean changed subtly as her gaze rested on the man finishing a business call via his cell phone. Mya witnessed that change, and understood what it meant. There was a bond between Elle and Oliver Cooper. He claimed he'd known it the first time he'd delivered her pizza. They'd both done everything they could to fight it, but in the end, love prevailed.

No one understood that better than Mya.

"Come down, Casper. Here, kitty, kitty," Cora crooned.

"That's obviously not working," Kaylie declared. At nearly seven, she was older and wiser, and made certain Cora knew it.

Sometimes the younger child accepted it. But not today.

"Quit bossing me," she said. "If it wasn't for me, your mommy would be dead."

Dear precious Kaylie accepted that. Watching Kaylie grow had given Mya something she'd lost during Elle's formative years. In essence, Cora and Kaylie were equally matched, and as close as sisters.

For months Dean, Mya and the doctors had scrambled to find Elle's perfect match. And then, just as all hope had seemed lost, the new drugs had started to work. Elle's condition improved. Remission occurred. All the while, another miracle was taking place. Elle's perfect match was discovered, not in her own daughter, or in her mother, father, uncles, cousins, strangers. Her perfect match had come along with the child Mya had been carrying without realizing it at the time. It seemed exhaustion and worry hadn't been the only reason for her queasiness and fatigue. She'd been pregnant. Baby Cora had been born screaming a month and a half early. Her umbilical cord had contained the stem cells that ultimately saved Elle's life.

Dr. Andrews had called it a miracle. Of course, Suzette had insisted it had all been predestined and written in the stars. It turned out Suzette finally met her match, too. The love of her life had been making a house call, but he'd been a plumber, not a doctor.

Mya saw more of Claire these days when she commuted to Brynn's twice a week. On those days she helped Claire,

who'd left her teaching job to take over the clothing bou
tique. Mya balanced the books, helped with the ordering
and whatever else needed to be done, but these days Brynn'
was more Claire's baby. Mya's passions lay here on her be
loved island, where it all began.

"Well?" Elle said as her young husband neared. "Who
was on the phone?"

There was no evidence of the nerd in Oliver these days
"You aren't going to believe it. Goldie just agreed to take the
part."

"Did I not tell you it would all work out?" Elle exclaimed

She and Oliver decided to help Kaylie and Cora get the
cat out of the tree. Dean went to get a ladder. And Mya
joined the others in the shade. They all peered up at the cat
heads tipped back, squinting at the sunlight filtering through
the leaves.

When Mya wondered about the authenticity of miracles,
she only had to look as far as her husband and their often-
times noisy family: Millie, Elle, Oliver, Kaylie and Cora.
She and Dean had argued about little Cora's name. In the
end, Mya had her way. He'd had his way plenty of other
times, evidenced by the size of her belly these days. They
hadn't planned to have another child. Of course, none of
their children had been planned. Surprises seemed to be
their specialty. Millicent told everybody that life had a way
of happening around Dean and Mya.

Mya didn't argue. At least not about that.

She couldn't help smiling a little at the sight of Dean trying to coax the cat down and everyone else yelling up their two-cents' worth. Bossiness ran in this family. She was hoping this baby was a boy for Dean, but if it was another girl, she knew he would simply add on to the playhouse castle he was building for his princesses. He would take it in stride the way they'd learned to take everything in stride.

There was a rhythm to their life, like the ebb and flow of the tide and the changing seasons. Sometimes subtle, sometimes harsh, the changes made life rich.

Life happened. She liked the sound of that.

* * * * *

Turn the page for another exciting NEXT read that will have all your friends talking.

A thousand goodbyes come after death—the first six
months of bereavement.
—Alan Gregg

The woman sat so still a casual onlooker might have
thought she was a statue. It was only when you looked more
closely that you could make out the faint rise and fall of her
chest. Her hands, with short, unpolished nails and long, el-
egant fingers, lay motionless on the arms of her wheelchair.

The only sound in the room were the muted tick of the
mantel clock and the occasional soft snore of the fat calico
cat that slept curled on the hearth.

The woman sat for a long time, just staring out the third-
story window that overlooked a narrow coastal road and af-
forded a magnificent view of the lichen-covered rocks and
gray, seething ocean beyond.

Today was a windy, overcast day, but at this time of year in this part of Northern California, most of them were. Occasionally, a shaft of sunlight appeared, but not often.

As she watched, a silver speck cut through the cloud cover. It was visible only a moment, just long enough to remind her that the outside world existed, no matter how much she tried to pretend it didn't.

Behind her, an elevator door slid open.

"Claire." A tall, stooped, older man walked into the room and placed his arthritic hand on her shoulder. "Alejandro is driving into town for supplies. Would you like to go along for the ride?"

"No, thank you, Uncle Richard."

"Claire, my dear, you haven't been out of this house all week. Don't you think—"

She shook her head. "I'm fine, Uncle Richard. Please don't worry about me." She still hadn't looked at him.

The old man seemed about to say something else, but then he simply sighed, his shoulders slumping in defeat. He would have given anything to bring some lasting happiness back into the world of his beloved niece. He'd have given his entire fortune. The past six years of his life. Anything. But nothing could give back to Claire what she had lost.

Sometimes he thought she might as well have died in the accident because everything that had made her uniquely

Claire had disappeared. All that joy, all that energy and enthusiasm—vanished as if it had never existed.

In her old life, she'd been a people person.

Now she was a recluse.

Richard Fitzhenry Sherman was eighty-five years old, and on days like this, he felt every one of them. "I'll be downstairs if you want me."

"All right."

When she heard the door close after him, and she knew she was once more alone, she removed her glasses and placed them on a nearby mahogany table. Then, wearily, she rubbed the bridge of her nose. This had been a rough week. One of those weeks when even the act of breathing seemed like too much effort.

She knew she was lucky, thanks to her uncle's money and influence. Another woman with lesser means wouldn't have been able to afford the extensive reconstruction surgery that had transformed her into a woman whose scars were no longer visible to the outside world.

Claire turned and wheeled herself over to her desk, which had been especially made to accommodate her chair. At the movement, Daisy, her cat, stretched and yawned, then settled back into sleep.

Claire looked at the screen of her computer monitor, which displayed a white screen filled with text. It was chapter twenty of her newest book in progress, and although she'd attempted to work all morning, she still hadn't written her daily quota of four new pages.

She knew exactly why she'd had so much trouble concentrating. She wondered if her uncle was aware of the significance of today's date. If that was why he'd seemed so especially concerned and solicitous today, even more so than usual.

Suddenly tears filled her eyes, which surprised her—for she prided herself on her calm acceptance of her life, particularly of the fact that she never allowed self-pity to undermine the peace she had achieved with such difficulty.

Six years ago.

Six years ago today.

The tears slid unchecked down her cheeks as memories engulfed her, memories of the day her life changed forever.

The adventure that was my life took another sharp turn that afternoon when I arrived at the high school to pick up my daughter, Trudy. I was congratulating myself on having managed to read a whole chapter in my college economics text without falling asleep when Trudy emerged from the band hall hand-in-hand with a tall, dreadlocked young guy with a number of tiny gold rings attached to his body—some of them in his ears.

I consider myself to be a "cool" mom. I do not overreact when my daughter decides she wants to dye her hair black or wear a dog collar. If she wants to experiment with vegetarianism, I will happily cook tofu and sprouts. I remember what it was like to be a teenager, trying to figure out what life is all about, and I promised myself that I would not be a smothering, overprotective, combative mother. I would strive to understand my daughter and help her through this passage in her life with love and compassion.

This is what I told myself. But all the talk in the world does not prepare you to see your *little girl* hand in hand with some freaky-looking *boy*. It was as if someone opened a trap door in my brain and swept every reasonable attitude out into space. Before I even knew what was happening, I was out of the car, glaring at that young man as if he was a grasshopper devouring my prize roses.

"Uh, Mom? Are you okay?" Trudy stopped a few feet from the car and frowned at me.

"Of course. I'm fine." I stared at their clasped hands. If I had had laser vision, they would have been sliced in two.

Mom-vision worked pretty well, though. Trudy dropped the boy's hand. "Mom, this is Simon."

"Hello, Simon." I tried to smile, but my face was frozen in an expression of menace. The best I could do was to try not to sound as horrified as I felt.

"Simon plays the clarinet."

The clarinet is such an ordinary instrument. Shouldn't a boy who looked like this play something more bizarre? "That's nice," I murmured. I was beginning to feel pretty ridiculous. I mean, up close the kid had zits and braces. Behind all the window dressing, he was just an ordinary boy.

"We're working on a duet for the concert next month."

Just when I was beginning to feel safe. My mother's voice

echoed in my head. *That better be all you're working on.* I coughed, choking on the words I refused to let pass my lips.

I grabbed Trudy's hand and pulled her toward the car. "Nice meeting you, Simon."

She waited until we were out of the parking lot before she spoke. "What was that all about?"

"What was what all about?" I pretended to concentrate on traffic, but out of the corner of my eye, I could see her pressed up against the passenger door, her arms hugged tightly across her chest.

"The way you acted with Simon back there. You were so rude."

"I was not rude. I was perfectly civil."

"Yeah, if you call *glaring* at someone civil. What was wrong with him?"

"You mean besides the fact that he has more holes in his head than Swiss cheese?" I was definitely channeling my mother now, but I couldn't stop myself.

"Mom! I can't believe you said that. What happened to all those speeches about tolerance and diversity? Besides, lots of people have piercings."

"We're not talking about other people. We're talking about the young man who was holding your hand."

"Oh, so that's it!" Trudy's voice was pitched higher than normal. "What's wrong with him holding my hand?"

Nothing. That's the answer I should have given her. The

answer the rational side of my brain knew was right. But that other part of my brain, the wild, irrational, fearful part, reminded me of every way I'd screwed up my life. I'd started out holding a boy's hand and a few years later I'd been sitting in the Planned Parenthood office, crying big fat tears and watching my dreams of college graduation and the life I'd always expected to have washing away. And I simply couldn't let my daughter make the same mistake.

Coming this September

In the first of Charlotte Douglas's Maggie Skerritt mysteries, an experienced police detective has to predict a serial killer's next move while charting her course for the future. But will Maggie's longtime friend and confidant add another life-altering event to the mix?

PELICAN BAY
Charlotte Douglas

REQUEST YOUR FREE BOOKS!

2 FREE NOVELS TO INTRODUCE YOU TO OUR BRAND-NEW LINE!

Ne^{xt}™

There's the life you planned. And there's what comes next.

HELL'S BELLES
by Kristen Robinette

An often funny, always compelling novel about the belles of a Southern town who are about to learn that sometimes dreams do come true…in the most unexpected ways.

Coming this October